A Witch's Penance

J.K. Divia

Paperback ISBN: 979-8-9875277-8-8
eBook ISBN: 979-8-9875277-7-1
Cover Design: Paper & Sage
Illustrations: Zooe Franci
Editing: Rosie Vox
Proofreading: by Chelsea McKenna

DEDICATION

To my family, especially my husband, for all his support and help in continuing to make this author dream of mine a reality. To my mother, who taught me what resilience and strength look like, and how to never give up. To the friends who encouraged me throughout this journey and pushed me to keep going. To everyone who was part of the *A Witch's Penance* writing process. To my cousin Todd and friend Jess for beta reading. To the early editors, my ARC readers, and fellow author friends. To my kids for being my sunshine on cloudy days. And finally, to my grandmother, who taught me to have faith, because God never gives us more than we can handle.

A Witch's Penance was inspired by my own journey through grief. While parts of this story are inspired by the Forfar witch trials in Scotland, all parts of this story are fictional and should not be taken as fact. This book is a work of fiction. All names, characters, businesses, events, and incidents are either a product of the author's imagination or used in a fictitious manner. Any resemblance to actual persons, living or dead, or actual events is purely coincidental.

This book deals with mental health and processing grief and trauma. If you or someone you know is struggling with their mental health, please reach out to your local resources. No one needs to struggle alone.

For Eloise and Nancy.

For mom and for myself.

PROLOGUE

They say that when a woman is pregnant, the baby's DNA flows through her bloodstream, absorbing into her own tissue and creating cellular threads that tie them both together. In most cases, the baby's DNA will eventually disappear from the mother's body. The babies, though, always carry with them their mother's blood. With this blood comes cellular memories passed down from generation to generation. The stories may be forgotten, but the pain lives on. Blood holds no secrets; the pain of our grandmothers becomes ours, and it will echo in the daughters who follow.

Chapter One

Rain Drops

It's raining outside. The soft fall of water promises to wash away the harshness of time, giving us the chance to start anew. Grandmother talks fondly about missing the sound of rain singing on a metal roof. She always says how there was nothing like it in the world to calm the mind and soothe the soul. The best sleep she ever had, she says, was when the rain sang to her from up above. She never stopped missing her tin roof or the way the rain played its melody, not even after her health declined to the point where she could no longer live in her old farmhouse alone. Not even when the only option was to move her hours away from her long-time home so that my mother could care for her.

It's one of the reasons I demanded a tin roof when we went house hunting all those years ago. We had just welcomed our first child, something I had longed for but hesitated over, always fearful that something terrible would happen. Fate, along with a family planning failure, took the decision out of my hands. Not long after we married, we were blessed with a baby girl, Audrey, with beautiful copper hair and an ever-present smile. But the sunshine she brought into our life also exacerbated the craze of city life, especially for me. The lines of mismatched brick walls in an endless maze of streets in Baltimore started to feel like they were closing in. When our son came two years later, I could no longer hide that I was drowning.

My husband Aaron, seeing my struggles, sold the red-brick row home we lived in and packed us up to the country. It was a place I promised would ease my anxieties, where I could keep it together and lessen his mental and financial load. A place where I wouldn't wake our daughter or our son every hour to make sure they were still breathing or wake him up to check on them just to be sure. It would be a place where I would lay them in their beds without the fear of imaginary stray bullets penetrating the walls and killing them, and where I could get my need to fill our stoop with delivery packages under control.

Aaron delivered on his end buying us a gorgeous colonial with bright yellow siding in a subdivision made to feel like country living—something he jokes I conjured out of thin air, given the state of the housing market in the area.

Grandmother laughs when we talk about our good luck finding the house. "When it's right, it's easy," she says, and I can't argue with her. Everything fell into place at the right time. No sooner had we decided to move than I ran into a neighbor I'd never spoken to before, someone I'd only chased out of my designated parking spot a few times in annoyance. What started as a friendly exchange turned into an unexpected conversation where I casually mentioned we were looking to sell our house. Immediately, he offered to buy it. He'd been looking for investment opportunities in our area for some time. I laughed, thinking he was joking, but he wasn't. A month later, he and Aaron, along with our lawyers, had worked out the sale. Not long after, we found our dream home. I try to push away the fear that something bad must happen to balance it out and just accept our good fortune.

Our new community was everything we had imagined; huge, wooded lots surrounded by farms, cul de sacs filled with children riding bikes and drawing with colorful chalk on driveways lined by bright yellow and white daffodils in the spring. Black and white patched Holstein-Friesian cows mooing good morning and evening in the not-so-distant fields surrounding us. A house where I could sit in my own floral recliner, one not yet faded by time and old memories, and sit next to our wood-burning fireplace, sipping hot black tea while listening to the rain sing on the tin roof overhead. A sturdy house where I could plant a garden and tend, barefoot, to the small plot of soil. A space for herbs, berry bushes, and vegetables. A garden like the one Grandmother Anne always spoke about from her childhood.

A place she said where she would walk into her garden with nothing but a salt and pepper shaker and eat lunch from the vines and grounds of the garden beds, a lunch as close to what the good Lord had intended for us to eat. A lunch I have not yet been brave enough to try. I can't shake the fear of worms and bugs that plague such gardens and the germs from the birds and animals that reside outside. But I do allow myself to feel grounded in the body of the earth, something I could never do in the city, at least not without worrying about stepping on dirty needles or broken glass. I let the soft blades of grass stick between my toes as I pad around the yard, smiling at the rare sight of fairy wings, what my grandmother calls the spider webs glistening with morning dew atop the grass.

Things are never truly easy, though. The dirt from the garden can only do so much. Sometimes, I still feel the intrusiveness of old fears flooding my mind. Now the fear of stray bullets is replaced by the fear of my car not being in park and rolling down our long, steep driveway, possibly hitting a neighbor or launching into the house directly across from us. Somedays, I can't make it to the front door of our house without going back multiple times to make sure the gear stick is still in park. My husband says it's like viewing a constant loop of a movie scene when he watches me through the front door camera on those days. The days when I can't remember, or lack faith in myself, that I correctly parked or locked the door.

The rain is one of the few things that can bring me out of such a loop. The way it falls from sky to earth like a calming shower, quelling my fears, even if only for a moment. The deep, earthy scent of it. The sound. Even the boom of thunder or crack of lightning will bring ease to the tension I hold inside me. Tension I work hard to hide. It's exhausting to be strong all the time.

The women in my family are all strong, proud, independent, and they always stop to watch the rain fall. It entrances us—the way it blurs the image of the outside world like a protective curtain, shutting out any danger. I sometimes catch my daughter Audrey watching me stare at the rain with mild curiosity, much like I watched my mother and grandmother when I was a child myself. I wonder how many generations of daughters have observed their mothers in the same way, like an unspoken tradition passed down without thought through the years. I wonder how far back that tradition goes, maybe all the way back to our ancestors in Scotland. To leave the only country you've ever known and start anew with nothing, that takes strength, faith, or at the very least, desperation.

The rain is a reminder that what's done is past, and it will wash away from memory.

Chapter Two

Marked for Beauty and Tragedy

The women who came before me were pillars of strength and faith. At one point in their lives, they were all beautiful. Each first-born daughter is marked with the signature dark auburn hair and light grey eyes. But unbroken? It's hard to say at what point they ever were. We are made to bear things that would break any normal person. To bear them in silence, internally. We go on, so the rest of the world never knows what horrors have befallen us and our families. It's made us sensitive to the vibrations of others, both the living and those who lie in the shadows. That's why we can hear the soft murmur of unspoken voices and see the shadows that lurk just beyond the corner of normal vision. People say sensitive souls have a gift, but when you live in fear of it, it feels more like a curse.

Grandmother Anne has never seen it that way. In my earliest memories of her, she's sitting in a faded floral recliner, her once auburn hair fading in streaks of grey. She would speak of blessings and people I barely knew or could never meet. When we, as children, came to her with complaints about the injustices of the world, she would often shake her head in disapproval at our "Why me?" cries and answer with a simple, "Why not you?"

I was raised to believe that is the strength of the women in our family: to ask, "Why not?" instead of "Why?" To grin and bear it. To carry on, not just for ourselves, but for our loved ones, who are our world. We carry on because we must. It is our duty to help others shoulder their sadness while we carry ours inside in silence. If I am being honest, sometimes it is easier to get lost in other people's grief than in my own.

Grandmother says we are worriers because we have big hearts; she says that is why I struggle with sadness and anxiety. But I know the truth. We worry because we know that bad things happen, and we have come to expect that they will happen again. Our family history has proved this generation after generation, all the way back to Scotland. Our ancestors braved a sea voyage, landing in the port of Baltimore in search of a better life, religious freedom, and a fresh start. Instead, she found more of the same struggles she had sought to escape, along with the isolation that comes from adapting to a new culture and dialect.

Every member of the family bears a scar, mental or physical, almost like a rite of passage or an initiation to adulthood. It passes from mother to child, regardless of gender. Car accidents are so frequent that sometimes I wonder if any of us should have licenses, despite the fact there has yet to be an accident where we were at fault— according to the police reports anyway.

Accidents and tragedies are part of our legacy: like the time my grandmother's cousin vanished without trace on her way home from work one night, never seen or heard from again. Or my great-uncle and his wife, who hydroplaned off a mountain road on the way to their honeymoon. A road that my mother's grandmother forbade anyone from driving down again. Now, it's a spot popular with ghost hunters and urban legend seekers hoping to catch a glimpse of their spirits.

From freak accidents to murders, disappearances, and just pure bad luck, every member of the family has been shaped by misfortune, haunted by the guilt of what they could have done differently. Grandmother calls it a trial, that we all must have our faith tested by the world. Her faith in God remains unwavering despite the many trials she has endured. Her commitment to prayer and faith are almost an obsession; she believes there is great power in the spoken words of her prayers.

I don't see it as a trial. I see it as a curse, one that claims both the young and old alike. A curse on which spoken words have no effect. Sometimes, I feel as though my trial never ended. At times, I forget. But then I hear the whisper of a shadow in the darkness, the outline of something lost standing in the corner of my dreams.

I fear for those who have yet to bear their scar and face their trial, that they will also survive what will haunt them if they do survive it. I pray my daughter will survive it when her time comes. Though not everyone does.

Chapter Three

Not Something I Can Help

"It's not something I can help. I come by it naturally. My mother killed herself, you know," Grandmother says as I hand her a fresh cup of tea with milk, watching her carefully for any signs of distress. I ask if she is feeling okay today. She doesn't visit often. It is a struggle for her to get in and out of the car and into the house with her walker, even with the metal ramp we installed for her. Usually, the sight of her great-grandchildren and great-grand-dog are enough to put her in the best of moods. Today, however, is different.

Today, she sits quietly in my recliner, gazing at the murder of crows frolicking and rolling down the hill in the front yard after the rain. The children fail to engage her and instead spend their time playfully attacking my mother. Cubby, our dog, lays lovingly at her feet like a black and white rug, keeping her company in silence while she stares off into the distance. There's a weight, a heaviness, about her.

Reaching up to the collar of her shirt, she

pulls out the old iron crucifix necklace, made from the nails of a horseshoe, a keepsake from our ancestor who brought it over from Scotland. It's something I've never seen her take off , and rarely does she expose it like this.

As I set the tea on the table beside her, she reaches out and takes my free hand.

"Sorry, Mom," she says, her gaze shifting to the photo frame on the wall, which contains individual portraits of our family's maternal line. The same one hangs at my mother's house. Grandmother gave it to me when my daughter was born, along with an emerald-green baby blanket that she had crocheted and got blessed at her church.

I feel Grandmother's melancholy swirling around me like a shadow, threatening to blanket me in the same sorrow that weighs on her. I glance around for my mother, but she's busy playing with my daughter and son; their laughter rings out across the house. Grandmother grips my hand tighter, despite its dampness, her lips forming a grim line and her light grey eyes now looking determined.

"I'm going to get a drink, Grandmother. Would you like anything?" I ask, trying to gently pull my hand away. But she holds on tighter. "Hey, Mom?" I call out, hoping to get her attention, but am met with silence as Grandmother's shadow deepens around me.

"Sometimes I wonder what I did to deserve everything that happened to me," Grandma says quietly, her voice heavy with years of unsaid pain.

I try to conjure up words of comfort, but nothing comes. She has never spoken like this before. I can't argue with her feelings, though. She has fought every single day of her life, never surrendering to the obstacles thrown in her path, always remaining positive and steadfast, determined to make the best of things. The saddest part of it all is that by the time she made it to retirement, her mind and body started to fail her, worn down by all the years of physical and mental stress. Saying goodbye to the house she had worked so hard for as a single mother with limited support, after my grandfather left, was one thing. But losing her independence and having to rely on her daughter was a bitter pill to swallow. Especially a lighthouse of a woman who had remained standing through every storm that had battered at her foundations.

"I look at you, your beautiful family, this beautiful house, and I wonder, what did you do to deserve all this?" she continues, gripping my hand with all her strength.

"I'm sorry, Grandma," I say softly, placing my hand over hers. "I don't know what I did either, but I'm happy you're here to enjoy it with us."

Letting go of my hand, she turns back to the window, muttering, "You must have been a saint in another life. Lord knows you weren't as a child." She sighs. "I do enjoy it here though, sweetie. Thank you for letting me come over, and for letting me see my angel babies. Where are they anyways?"

"Mom?" I call again, my voice louder this time.

"What, what do you want?" my mother calls from the next room, mock annoyance in her tone. "Can't you see I'm a little busy?" Finally, she waddles in, a child wrapped around each leg, their giggles filling the air.

It's starting to rain again, just a drizzle, and Grandmother releases her hold on me, sinking back into the comfort of the recliner, no longer so rigid. She turns her head to watch the ruckus the children are causing, her face breaking into a wide grin.

"You okay, Mother?" Mom calls out, concern edging her voice.

"Me? Oh, yeah, I'm fine. Just wondering where my angel babies were," Grandmother says, her voice light. "But I am getting tired. If you're ready, I'd like to go."

She still smiles, but her tea remains untouched. The dark clouds that had hovered over her moments ago seem to have passed. It's only been an hour, but her visits have become shorter and shorter in recent months as her stamina continues to decrease.

My mother begins to shake off the children, much to their delight.

"A little help here, please! These monsters won't let go!" she says playfully, but I hear tension in her voice that wasn't there before.

I untangle my son from her leg, pretending to nibble on his belly before grabbing my daughter too and pulling her in as she tries to dart past.

The children dutifully give hugs and kisses goodbye as Mother and Grandmother prepare to leave. I follow them out.

"We'll talk later," my mother whispers in my ear as she pulls out of my hug, moving to open the door for Grandmother.

I watch from the door as they slowly make their way down the drive from the door. Grandmother stops midway and looks up at the sky, rain lightly falling on her face. For a moment, she closes her eyes. I wonder what she's thinking.

Then, she slowly exhales, turns toward the window to look at me, makes the sign of the cross, blows me a kiss, and shuffles toward the car.

Chapter Four

What's Passed Down

"It's not something I can help. I come by it naturally."

I've always found this unnerving when Grandmother says it. She started saying it more often since having a series of mini-strokes over Christmas four years back.

Christmas was once her favorite holiday. Now, not even the smell of cookies baking, or a drive around the wealthy neighborhoods or local topiary gardens to admire the twinkling lights and festive displays can summon the joy she once felt for the season. Now, we often find her gazing down at her wrinkled, knotty hands, clenched together on a plaid throw blanket. She sits quietly, tears welling in her foggy grey eyes as she looks up at the photos of family members lining her living room wall, her fingers curling around the old iron cross that's been passed down through the generations. At least, that's the story we've been told. No one really knows where the cross came from, just that it's been in our family for as long as anyone can remember. It's passed down to each first-born daughter by her mother, as both a rite of passage and a symbol of being the family matriarch. Grandmother received hers after her mother died, but she broke tradition by never passing it down to my mother. A small part of me wonders if it's because she knows deep down that it carries something dark with it. After all, it was still covered in my great-grandmother's blood when the coroner handed it to her.

Grandmother's moods have become increasingly melancholy, but if anyone has a right to sadness, it's her. She has endured the most suffering in our family. Sometimes I wonder if that is simply the result of being the oldest living member, the one who has seen it all. She has witnessed the death of her parents, siblings, a child, and a grandchild. Our relationship has always been strained. She used to say we fought so much because we were too alike, always vying for control over every little thing—from the clothes I wore to the books I read and the activities I participated in. I refused to learn the recipes

that were passed down to her, like special cookies and cakes, or home remedies like ginger and
milk tea, or a soup that would kill a flu dead in
its tracks. My brother Joseph, on the other hand,
was always eager to help her in the kitchen. He
would chide me for arguing with Grandmother
and tell me to show some empathy for all she had
been through, for all she had done for us after
our father left us for the bottle. Joseph was the
light of our family, a favorite of both mine and
Grandmother's. My mother would call him the
mayor of our community, since she couldn't even
go to the grocery store without someone asking
if she was Joseph's mom. After he passed, Grandmother spent less and less time in the kitchen,
often complaining about how the rest of us, especially me, didn't give a damn about preserving
the family traditions she worked so hard to pass
down.

As I've grown older, my empathy toward
her has replaced the indignities of my childhood,
like the favoritism I clearly saw her shower my

brother with. How annoyed I would get when she would make me stop what I was doing and wait on my brother, bringing him a drink or something to eat. Now, I wish he was still here for me to care for, and that I had paid more attention to the recipes she can no longer remember. Recipes my brother cannot share, and that I can't pass down. Recipes I search the internet for, but never come close to tasting the same as what she made. My mother, not being much of a cook, never learned them either. Even the lamb cake Grandmother used to make for Easter every year. My brother and I would pretend to sacrifice the lamb, fighting over who got to "slit" its throat with a butter knife. The cake always crumbles when I try to recreate it.

In her ninety-two years, Grandmother has lost so much: both her parents before she even turned thirty, a brother, a child, and a grandson. She almost died herself once. In fact, she was supposed to. After a car accident, she was in a coma for two months. Her husband, who was driving, collided with a cattle car, with four young chil-dren in the back seat, all injured.

My mother was just eight years old when they brought her in to say goodbye to her mother. She had her own injuries, and she had told the doctors that the woman with the shaved head and multiple tubes sticking out of her was not her mother. I can't imagine what that would look like to a child. But I do know what it's like to be a mother with young children in a bad accident. My daughter was ten months old when we hit a stag and totaled our new van. By the grace of God, or maybe Grandmother's prayers, none of us were injured. The stag, much to the shock of the police officer who came to help us, walked away from the wreck. Our daughter, secured in her car seat, slept through the whole thing.

Grandmother's family was not as lucky. The accident that put her in a coma left her with the worst injuries. They said she was brain-dead, and it was time to let her go. But when they took her off life support, she woke up a few days later.

They called it a miracle. She attributes it to her aunt, who came every day to pray and read to her when everyone else had given up. On days like today, when not even the sound of falling rain can soothe her soul, I wonder if it was a curse that kept her alive to suffer through so much more.

The photo Grandmother stares at most often is a large, wooden-framed collage of four black-and-white portraits. It holds the first-born women of our family going back four generations, starting with her mother and ending with me. All of us share the same smooth, pale skin covered in freckles and large, round eyes.

My mother and I often start with her grandparents when discussing the family curse. The first woman in the frame is my great-grandmother. Her ending was not a happy one; in her grief, she passed down a legacy to my grandmother along with the iron nail cross necklace. Within a year, at the age of twenty-one, Grandmother had married, with both her parents in attendance, and then became pregnant with my mother. Before my mother was born, both her parents were gone, what the coroner ruled a murder–suicide. The police suspected it was due to jealousy over an affair, and my grandmother believed them, but others, both in town and in the family, suspected robbery. Given the rumors, I believe that theory. Some said my great-grandfather, a man otherwise seen as good, had been using his position at the post office to run a bootlegging operation on his farm. In the small mountain town where they lived, gossip spread fast, and some people believed there was a large sum of money hidden there. Within months of the rumors starting, my grandmother's cousin found my great-grandmother's body in the house. Within the hour, he found my great-grandfather hanging like a broken limb from a storm in a tree out back. The police couldn't confirm whether anything had been taken, but there was talk that some men had tried to shake down my great-grandparents, both of whom were formidable and stubborn in their own rights.

For a long time, we thought that was the start of it all. But once my mother began digging deeper into our family history, it became clear that whatever lurked in our lineage had been there far longer. A little girl crushed by a runaway workhorse. A young man caught in a barn fire when that same horse knocked over an oil lamp. Strange accidents that claimed lives and shattered families. Some of these stories were hard to come by, no doubt due to the superstitions that run deep in our family, the fear that speaking of such tragedies would invite more. Instead, we're left with news articles, death certificates, and speculation. I hold onto their stories though, grieving for ancestors I've never met, imagining their last moments, how they felt, and what they might have thought. Their stories play like memories in my mind.

It's easy to ask, "Why me?" In our family, the question is, "Why not?" We reason that bad things happen to people all the time, that we are no different. That it's simply luck of the draw, no one's fault and no one to blame. That

God never gives you more than you can handle. We say, "Better us than someone else." We carry it inside and push forward with our heads held high. I look up at the black-and-white photos in my entryway, of the women in our family line. I've never noticed before how we all have the same bob haircut in the photos. The last photo is mine. I know that one day, my daughter's picture will join the rest, and I worry that she'll ask, "Why not me?" I worry she'll look up at the line of colorless photos and feel as though she's destined to bear witness to the strength and tragedies of those who came before her. I worry she'll carry the pain, the fear, passed down to her from me and all the other women before her. And I worry what will happen when Grandmother and Mother are no longer here to pray for us, when the old iron cross and the family's fate lie in my hands. I wonder if my words will have the same power, or if, like Grandmother, I'll only have the strength to wait for the rain to offer some relief.

Chapter Five

Curses and Genealogy

I look at the photos of the women who came before me as I sit in my floral recliner, still warm from when Grandmother sat in it. The flesh of my arm begins to jiggle annoyingly as the phone vibrates beneath it.

"Hi, Mom," I answer.

"Hi, baby. Sorry about today. You know how your grandmother can be, and she's only getting worse. Are you okay?"

"Yeah, I'm fine," I say, tugging at a strand of hair and giving it a slight pull.

"Are you sure? You looked upset."

"No, just worried about Grandmother. She was saying some strange things . . . like she doesn't know what she did to deserve what happened to her. Almost like she was jealous or something. I've never heard her talk like that. Usually, she says, 'God never gives us more than we can handle,' and that we're blessed."

"Well," my mom sighs, "she's getting old, honey, and health-wise, she's not doing well. She keeps saying she feels tired. She's started talking about giving away some of her things, like her cookbooks and nativity collection. I think you need to start mentally preparing for her to pass. She might be preparing herself, too. I don't want to freak you out, but . . . she mentioned giving you the cross."

"What?"

"I know. But she seems to really want you to have it, and I think it would make her happy if you accepted it graciously. You don't have to wear it, except when she's around, to make her happy. You can keep it in a box for safekeeping, and when Audrey's old enough, pass it down to her."

"It should go to you," I say, tugging my hair tighter until I feel the soothing pressure on my scalp.

"She wants it to go to you, honey," she says firmly.

The thought of passing it down to my daughter sends a shudder through me. Grandmother always treated the cross as though it carried some sort of protection and responsibility.

Considering my great-grandmother was wearing it when she died, I can't help but feel the opposite.

"Eh, I don't know about that," I mutter.

"It's a family heirloom, Nina. It should be passed down. Your grandmother always said it carried good luck, that it was imprinted with the prayers and wishes for the future of the women who came before us. That it helped our ancestors cross the sea safely to America."

"Do you really believe that, Mom?"

"Well, I know there have been a number of times your grandmother should have died but didn't. And there have been moments, even in my own life, when terrible things happened, and I came out okay. There were times, looking back, when I can see that I was spared from something much worse. Have faith, Nina. Maybe it's what's been protecting us from this curse you keep talking about."

She ends the call with an "I love you," and I sit there, staring once again at the photo of the women who came before me.

I wish I knew for certain that I could protect my daughter with this cross. I would give it to her now if I could. I wish I could know that I was protected, and that she would be spared from the darkness that casts its shadow over our family. We aren't the first to suggest a curse, my mother and I. Every time I've opened up to a friend about our family history, they gasp and say we sound cursed. The first time I brought it up to my mother, she laughed it off, saying maybe they were right. But we've always daydreamed together about ways to break it.

I don't want to worry about my children's curses, but I can't help it. There's a certainty in my thoughts that I can't push away. My mother says that by obsessing over it, I'll somehow will it into existence and ensure their place in our family line of tragedies. That I'm creating a self-fulfilling prophecy by expecting something bad to happen. My husband agrees with her. He says I need to find a hobby, an outlet to distract my brain from these worst-case scenarios. A suggestion my mother echoes.

Mother has already found her outlet: genealogy. She's been building our family tree for years, always trying to get me involved in her little passion project. She spends hours in her home office, sorting through digitized archives and records. It's never really interested me, except for the interesting tidbits, like some ancestors getting fined for fornicating in a barn or being scalped at a fort in the wilderness. That was until she shared the discovery that our lineage traces directly to the Bruce clan of Scotland. I knew my grandmother's maiden name was Bruce, and that our ancestor had come to America through Baltimore, but I'd never heard of the clan connection.

I'd always been drawn to Scotland, its mythology, its culture. I grew up watching shows about sword-wielding Highlanders and mystery shows about Loch Ness. I felt a rush of excitement, followed by sadness, when my mother mentioned that one of the Bruce women had been accused of witchcraft during the Forfar witch trials in the 1700s. I'd read about the witch trials in Salem and had gone through a phase of watching shows about witches, even wishing I could be one, solving problems with protection spells and potions. But when my friends in high school started practicing with tarot cards and Ouija boards, I was filled with fear, as if I were in danger. The shadows that have always lurked in the periphery of my sight and mind seemed to be calling. Just being in the same room with those objects would send me spiraling into recurring nightmares for weeks.

When my mother mentioned Elspet's name, the accused Bruce woman, I felt a strange, inexplicable connection. Her name resonated with me in a way I can't explain. I want to imagine her like this—big round eyes, a small turned-up nose, hair falling in long, dark auburn waves down her back, hiking proudly through fields of heather, holding up tartan skirts like a romanticized heroine. But when I see her, I also see dark clouds unfurling and reaching out like tentacles to grab her. I see a look of desperation and fear behind a stoic face as she stands in a field of decaying earth.

"She's it!" I tell my mother, my voice rising.

"She's what?" my mother asks, confused.

"The source of our curse," I say.

Laughing, she replies, "Well, I can't find a direct connection to her yet, or how she fits into our family tree. All I know is she was a Bruce. But I guess what better source of a curse than an accused witch from a witch trial?"

It isn't that I wish we had someone or something to blame, as much as I wish there was a curse to break. Because then, I'd have some control over fate, over destiny. I could banish the shadows that have haunted me since childhood when my brother died in an accident twenty-five years ago, something I will never forgive myself for. The rest I inherited in the womb. If there were someone to blame for our constant misfortunes, if there were a curse, then maybe I could spare my daughter, and my son. I could cure my family. I could cure myself from bringing about further heartbreak.

Sometimes I worry about how long I can keep it in, the sadness, the worry, the desperate need to control everything. I pray for strength, for forgiveness. Sometimes I feel as if I'm too far gone for God to hear me, for Him to forgive me for my childhood transgressions. I wonder if it will all be too much one day, as my mind slips with age, and disease, just like my grandmother's. I hear her words spill out when I visit her. *I come by it naturally, I can't control it.* Her dementia only exacerbates her sadness. She's so different now from the person everyone knew. A woman as bright as sunshine, with a permanent devilish glint in her eye. Now I understand what it took for her to keep that mask up all those years, to keep our family ghosts at bay. I could always see through her mask, even as a child. I resented it then, but now I understand it.

On the days it feels too much, and I'm on the verge of being overtaken by shadows, I thank God for the rain. Or for the blessing of a large walk-in shower with a rainfall showerhead. On heavy days, I sit on the white-and-black tile floor and let the steaming water fall on me, soothing, promising to wash away the pain. When I get out, I'll be renewed. When my daughter seems overwhelmed, I take her in with me, showing her how to let the water soothe her as it falls on her head. When the warm summer rain falls, I take the kids outside. I watch the raindrops fall on the green buds in my garden, springing back to life. I watch my children's heads fill the air with infectious giggles as they spin and run in the rain. The damp, musty smell of the earth is intoxicating as I step out from the overhang of my doorstep and welcome the splatter of droplets on my skin.

These moments of peace are fewer and farther between lately. The old fears creep back in, repackaged as new ones. My husband wants me to talk to someone about my fears, but that has never been easy for me. I've tried, God knows I have. I have picked up the phone, dialed the number only to fall mute when there was an answer at the other end. The one time I managed to speak up and tell a nurse how I was feeling a few months after my daughter was born, she assured me it would get better and the anxiety I was feeling was normal. To give birth to a child is to break off and expose a piece of you, of your soul. To make yourself more vulnerable because that piece of you is no longer safely held inside. It is unprotected in the world, and it leaves you open to experience immense joys, but also pain. There is no return to normal after that.

I promised my husband I would try again, and I've started to write as an outlet. This was encouraged by my mother—she says I've always been a storyteller. That I would write plays for the neighbor kids and I to act out for her and the other parents when I was young. I don't really remember though; it's been so long, and those memories have faded into the background as other ones have grown stronger and moved to the forefront.

My husband bought me a new laptop which I've dedicated to writing, supporting me as he has always done. From the moment we met, he became my rock, a steady, calming presence in my life. He was the one place where I could escape the noise and chaos of the world outside, and the dark paths in my mind. I was drawn to him instantly. A chance encounter at a dive bar in the city. I was out with friends, and he was there with his. When he walked in and approached the bar to order a drink, I felt his presence immediately. The dim bar lights seemed to cast an ethereal glow around him, pulling me toward him. I hadn't the nerve to go up to him, but much to my horror and gratitude, a friend did it for me. From then on, I knew he was exactly what I wanted, what I needed. The light surrounding him drew me in, like a moth to a flame.

My husband has never been one for grand gestures or extravagant gifts. He doesn't shower me with trinkets or flowers, but he has an incredible ability to give me exactly what I need, exactly when I need it. His gifts are often small, but carry deep meaning, like a key to his apartment tucked inside a card, picking up dinner and a sweet when I've had a rough day, or more recently, this laptop. He has encouraged me to channel my fears and anxieties onto paper, helping me distance them from our reality. While I tend to worry and obsess over the future, my husband remains grounded in the present, always focused on tangible solutions that can be enacted right now. We couldn't be more different in the way we think, and while it has been a source of contention in our relationship at times, it has never been an obstacle to our love. I show him how to dream and he keeps me grounded.

I've started to type a story on the gift he gave me. I wasn't sure what about at first. I would open the document and stare at the blank page until suddenly, my fingers began to dance across the keyboard. After a few paragraphs, it became clear that it would be about Elspet. Even if I don't have proof of a direct connection to her, I can't help but feel that there is one.

Since discovering her name, there has

been this deep, strong pull to her. She haunts my thoughts and lingers in the background of my mind, like a cat slinking behind the furniture of a cluttered room. Even the shadows that usually plague my mind have made way for her. Maybe if I get her out of my head and onto paper, I can move on from her, and from our family curse. Maybe with enough research, I can prove to everyone the curse is real and break it. For as long as I can remember, I've played every possible scenario for every situation in my head. I've always considered it one of my strengths, while others have called it an illness. I know I can use it to save my family by looking at every possible path of Elspet's story and find where the answer to our curse lies. I can use it to free my family. I can free myself, and be the daughter, the wife, and the mother my family deserves. After all, there is no God without the Devil. There has to be light to recognize the dark, and sometimes you need a little more than just prayers. Sometimes, you follow up, "Why not me?" with "Never again."

CHAPTER SIX

THE STORY OF ELSPET BRUCE

Rain to summon my love

I t was raining, as it often does in the little Scottish market town of Forfar and the surrounding farms and villages in early spring. The rain was quite often a burden, bringing with it the difficulties of maneuvering in thick mud and muck. Many struggled with getting warm from the chill, and as it settled in their bones they wished for the warmer months of late April and May, which would soon be upon them. For Elspet Bruce, though, the rain brought with it a fire. One that burned deep and fierce inside her. The rain meant that she was free to escape the boredom of the cramped, cold stone house that lay a few miles outside town, where she lived with her sister Mary and the rest of their family. The rain brought with it a dark grey curtain of privacy. A chance to run to her secret meeting spot with the neighboring stable boy, Tomas. The rain would obscure the view of her mother's ever-watchful eye as she snuck out to the barn. The hard pitter patter of its droplets would cover up any noises that escaped from the young lovers' lips during their meetings tangled in the thick yellow straw. Elspet did not just welcome the rain, she prayed for it. If she knew of a way, she would forsake the sunshine and summon the precious drops from the darkened sky each and every day. Such was her love for Tomas, a man who had promised to marry her once his fortunes changed and he could afford to properly keep a wife and family. Elspet did not care for luxuries though; as the daughter of a protestant priest in a still largely Catholic country, she was accustomed to doing without. She would tell Tomas that she only cared for him and not earthly goods, but he would not be persuaded.

Her days were filled with the agony of waiting for her true love when there was no rain in sight, and she would look out her window to the white clouds and will them to turn to darkness and bring down the water to free her. Days when the roses stood straight and proud under the warm sunlight breaking through the clouds at the front of their grey stone house drove her to madness.

Elspet spent her days working in the side garden bed, filled with herbs that she was learning about from Mistress Agnes, one of the midwives outside of town and her mother's sister. Mistress Agnes followed the old ways, making medicines for the townspeople from the fruit of her garden. These ways, though, had become increasingly met with suspicion and distrust by the prominent men in the village.

Elspet's mother frequently reassured her that, despite her modest background, her pretty face would likely lead her to securing a good marriage, one where she would not be forced to tend to gardens like her aunt. Her mother was always concerned with such things, whereas Elspet and Mistress Agnes were not. Sometimes Elspet felt as though she should have been born to Agnes instead. Agnes possessed a warmth that her mother did not. She thought it strange that a woman married to a priest would be so concerned with status as her mother was. Elspet did not care though, she longed to marry Tomas. Her mother would never approve of a match with a man of so little. She was content to live a harder life where she would work to make her own comfort, rather than be without love and kept like a caged bird in the house of a wealthy man. She would work as a healer, like her aunt, carrying on the old ways. Mistress Agnes was respected by the older townsfolk, at least one woman in each generation of her family had been cunning folk and kept to the old ways. The knowledge had been passed to Agnes and Elspet believed her mother harbored some jealousy over that.

As the older folk in town began to die and the religious whim of kings changed, so did the respect for her and people like her. Fear and suspicion seeped in and unusual knowledge of plants for healing began to make people wary. Of course, those who began to look at her with suspicion still came to her when faced with illnesses that prayer and faith could not cure alone. But even as public feeling changed, Elspet remained steadfast. She had always drawn to her aunt; she remembered her mother bringing her and her sister to her house for medicines when they were young, or when her mother had errands to run. Though she had a sharp wit and propensity for speaking in a blunt manner, Agnes always met them with a kind eye. When Elspet was old enough to gain the freedom of wandering her family's farm, her mother allowed her to visit her aunt's cottage. Over the years, Elspet's visits became more and more frequent until, one day, Agnes decided it was time to put her niece to use.

Thanks to the healing wisdom Mistress Agnes was teaching her, she would be a proper wife to Tomas no matter where they lived. She would be free and able to care for and help support the family she knew in her heart they would build.

When Elspet wasn't occupied with learning from Agnes, she would look up at the sky begging for her tear drops on the dry earth to turn to rain. She would not smile again until the roses in the front garden began to fill and fall under the weight of the raindrops. Until the smell of the dewy earth called her and Tomas forth to join as one again.

Chapter Seven

Whiskers on Feral Kittens

"What's wrong?" my husband asks, his voice laced with concern. I tighten my grip on the phone as I try to calm my mother through her broken sobs.

"Okay," I say, my voice steady, though my heart is racing. "I'll be there soon."

The phone hits the counter harder than I intended. I quickly check for any new cracks in the screen, then shove it into my pocket. Running a hand through my long, dark auburn hair, I begin twisting a large strand around my finger, taking a moment to collect myself. I need to be strong. I need to shoulder her grief and help her through this, just as she has done for me, for our family, countless times before.

Our family is matriarchal, built on the backs of the first-born women of each generation. This has created a bond between my mother and me that no one else quite understands. Only we can carry the weight of the family burdens, only we can be the emotional support for everyone else. But that bond doesn't extend to my grandmother. Where my mother has always tried to balance helping others with taking care of herself, Grandmother Anne pushed self-sacrifice to the extreme, even to the point of exhaustion or self-destruction.

I let out a breath I didn't realize I was holding as my husband's hand rests on my shoulder. The warmth radiates through me, releasing some of the tension I didn't even know I was carrying. I melt into his arms as he pulls me in for a hug. I wish I could stay there forever, hidden from the world.

"What happened? Is your mom okay?" he asks, his voice soft. He's always been adept at reading the subtle shifts in our faces, in our voices, in our emotions. He would scoff if I called him an empath, dismissing it as nonsense. He's a man of science, of facts, of data.

"No," I sigh, pulling out of his embrace and once again twisting a strand of hair around my finger.

He gently grabs my hand, untangling it from my hair, and places both hands on my arms, turning me to face him. I begin to calm under his touch.

"Her neighbor knocked on the door and told her he found her cat in the street," I say, my voice tight. "It's been run over."

"Oh God, again? Your poor mom." He pulls me into another hug, and I bury my face in his shoulder, inhaling the comforting scent of him.

"I know. Second cat in two years," I mumble, my words muffled.

"She has to find a way to keep them inside."

My mother's house could pass for a witch's cottage, a charming white Cape Cod with well-maintained garden beds and old silver maple trees scattered across the property. It's nestled on a crowded street in an overdeveloped town that it doesn't quite fit in with. I've never wondered why stray animals always find their way to her. Her home is a sanctuary, a haven for birds, bees, and the occasional stray cat. She has a connection with animals that most people don't, including me.

"Both cats were strays," I say. "They always found a way to slip out through the door."

"How's your grandma taking it?" he asks.

"I haven't asked Mom yet. I'm not sure it's worth it for her to tell her. She'll just forget anyway."

I take one last deep breath in the safety of his arms before pulling away to grab my purse. I dig through the clutter of candy wrappers and fruit snack packages until I finally find my keys, cursing under my breath as I do. After a few frustrating minutes, I head out the door and toward my dark blue SUV.

It's been a rough year for Mom. In addition to my grandmother's medical episodes, she lost her favorite cat, a black stray she had taken in. Or rather, it had adopted her. The cat appeared on her doorstep one day: a shaggy, pure black thing with yellow eyes, meowing insistently until she finally let it in. From that moment on, the cat, whom she named Attila the Hunny, made itself a fixture in her life. Every morning, it would follow her out the front door as she left for work at the local vet clinic. And every evening, it would wait for her under the old silver oak tree in the front yard, its tail swishing as she drove in. She would greet the cat first, then sometimes give a playful hello to the tree she'd adorned with a ceramic face. After a scratch behind the ears, Attila would follow her inside for the night. That was their routine for seven years. We used to joke that it was her familiar, the way it waited and seemed to understand her. She would laugh and ask, hands on her wide hips, if we were accusing her of being a witch. "If the broom fits!" Grandmother would always call out from her lift chair, before dementia stole her sense of humor.

It's a strange thing, watching your parents grieve. I had never seen my mother cry so hard as she did the day Attila was killed, not even when my brother died. I went with her to pick the cat up off the road, watching as she gently wrapped its broken body in a bath towel, then placed it in a box to take to the vet for cremation. I helped her pick out a tree, a pussy willow, under which she could bury its ashes in the yard.

As I pull into the driveway now, I see the flash of a small, dark shape darting from my line of sight. My stomach turns, and for a moment, I just sit there, breathing deeply, trying to steady. It's not the first time I've seen a shadow like that. Sometimes, even months after Attila's death, I swear I can still see him sitting under that same tree.

About six months after Attila passed away, another stray arrived, a short-haired dark grey cat with green eyes. Mom resisted at first, trying to shoo it away. But the cat was insistent, knowing she needed him. "God always sends you what you need," I told her, echoing the words she and Grandmother always said to me. Finally, she relented, opened the door, and said, "Come on, then." She named him Angus.

I take a final breath, steadying myself, before I get out of the car. The air feels bitter as I walk to the sidewalk and knock on her door. After a few moments, it opens, revealing her tear-streaked face, her eyes red and swollen. Without a word, I wrap her in my arms, and we cry together. Angus was with her for less than a year before he, too, met the same fate as Attila. Mom swears he will be the last one, that her heart can't bear the pain of losing another animal. I hope she changes her mind, though. I know she will feel empty without her furry companion waiting for her on the porch when she gets home tomorrow. I try to offer comfort, telling her that everything happens for a reason, but it's hard to reason the death of loved ones.

Chapter Eight

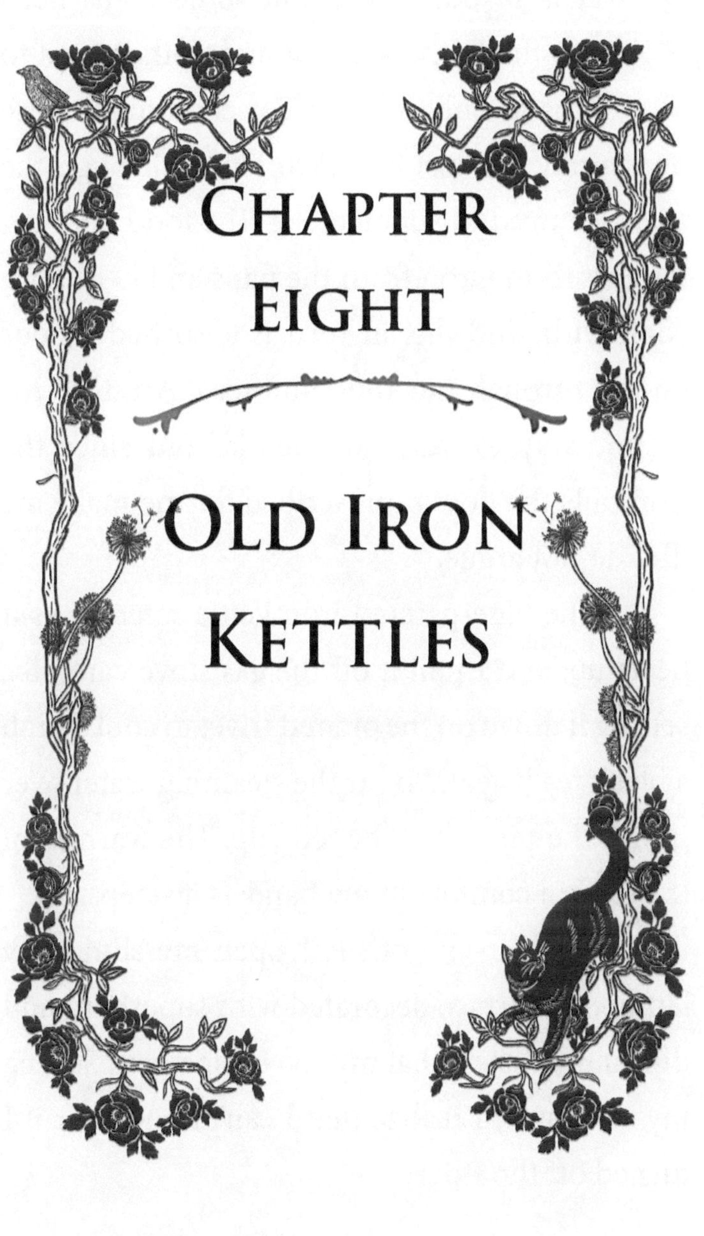

Old Iron Kettles

Iron is in our blood, but some of us need more than others. My grandmother used to tell us to only use iron for cooking because our family has lost so much blood through the ages, we need to supplement. The food and water absorb the iron from the pans and kettles we cook with, and this in turn is absorbed by our bodies through our food and teas. A rather romantic way to describe anemia, and since the iron pills the doctor prescribed for me make me ill, I do not argue.

The blue-painted iron kettle screams as it heats up, and I pull it off the gas stove carefully, setting it down on the old red trivet to cool. I grab a black tea bag and pour the steaming water over it into the pumpkin-shaped cup. The warmth of the tea is a comfort in my hand as it steeps.

Once in my office, I open my slim, grey laptop, its surface decorated with superhero and dinosaur stickers that my son slapped on. Setting my tea down, I realize that I can't remember if I turned off the stove.

I think I turned it off. I did, didn't I?

I pause, then smell the air. No gas. If I didn't turn it off, though . . . I could blow up the house.

I go back and forth in my mind, the nagging thought growing louder, until I can't ignore it any longer. I stand and run downstairs into the kitchen to check, just to make sure.

I check the burner for a dark blue flame, but it isn't there. I turn the knob one more time, ensuring it's all the way off, even though the burner is cool and there's no smell of gas.

The house is quiet. The kids are at daycare, and my husband is at work. I've taken a "sick" day from my own job as a scheduler for the hospital, though I feel guilty. I'm lucky to work from home, after all.

I bring up the story of Elspet and reread what I've written so far. She's waiting for her love. It sounds like a happy story—romantic, if nothing else. A woman and a man, bound in an ill-fated love, waiting to share an illicit kiss. The image in my mind is not unlike the covers of romance novels I'd see scattered around the house when I was growing up, the ones my mother read. But where does it go wrong? Where does it turn from a romantic story into one of horror? Where and when does my family fall into a long line of generational curses?

My mother's research has helped place the setting and mood of my story, but the rest is lost to history. Much of what I've found myself is based on speculation—rumors and whispers, old tales that contradict each other. Still, I can't stop thinking about Elspet. I can't stop thinking that whatever happened to her caused all our misfortune.

I wish I had a sign that I am on the right path.

Elspet, come to me. Show me. I repeat the words in my head, over and over, desperate for something to guide me.

Taking a sip of tea turns into a bath as I somehow miss my mouth, and tea comes rushing down my chin and neck. "Goddammit." I slam the cup down on the desk, spilling some tea on the edge of the keyboard. My frustration shifts into anger, and then, almost immediately, my mood shifts again. I turn the mug, and that's when I'm reminded of my mother's encouragement.

The mug is black, with bold white writing that says "Author". A recent gift from her. She was so excited when I asked her to dig deeper into Elspet and our family's history. I was happy to see her excitement, to see the dark clouds that hung over her after the passing of her cat, Angus, finally parted a little. She found most of the articles online after paying for access to old archives. I offered to pay her back for the fee, but she insisted it was for her own enjoyment as much as it was to help me.

One of the things she found was a woman named Helen, who had confessed to being a witch. Just hearing her name made my blood run cold. I felt it deep in my soul, like someone stepping on my grave. Helen was described as a bitter, mean drunkard, a town pariah, and according to the old papers, she'd confessed to all sorts of horrific deeds: sinking ships, defacing tombs, even cannibalism. She seemed eager to drag others down with her, including women like Elspet.

If Elspet was a witch, maybe the women in my family are too. Witchcraft wasn't always about casting spells back then; it was about being different. Our family has always been different, a little odd. We say and see things that make others uncomfortable.

Grandmother always talked about having "feelings", premonitions about bad things before they happened. From itchy palms signaling money coming or going, to hearing a loved one's voice calling for help when they were in trouble. Her "feelings" were always right. When I was eighteen, she called me to ask where I was. When I told her I was with friends, headed to another friend's house, she said she had a feeling and I needed to come home.

I laughed it off. But sure enough, an hour later, I ended up breaking my nose during a trampoline incident when an attempted backflip ended with my knee connecting with my face.

The morning of my car accident, I missed a call from her. Later, I found a voicemail, just her voice, asking me to be careful.

We're told that witchcraft is evil, that it'll send you to Hell. But what is witchcraft, and what is just a gift you're born or blessed with?

Back in Elspet's time, witchcraft was anything in a woman that strayed from piety, domestic skills, and obedience. God forbid she had any bad luck, or marks on her body, like moles or scars. By those standards, our family would've been accused. By my skin alone, spotted and scarred—I'd have been damned.

And while we're not casting spells or riding brooms, I can't deny that our family has a heightened sensitivity to things others don't notice. Though I don't share Grandmother's premonitions, I often find my senses heightened when it comes to smells, sounds, sights, things that others can't detect.

As a child, it terrified me, the shadows of people in the room that disappeared when I turned on the lights. The impish faces in the woodgrains of the wall or marble of the shower tiles. It still scares me sometimes. I remember asking Grandmother why the shadows followed me, why I couldn't escape them. She told me they attached themselves to people like us, and that I should firmly tell them to leave when I got too frightened. If that didn't work, then I should pray.

I tried, but I never could muster the strength in my voice for them to listen.

Grandmother would get frustrated with me when I woke her in the night, afraid of the shadows. She'd scold me, walking me back to my room in her old cotton muumuu, saying, "Child, I told you what to do. I cannot help you until you believe it."

Eventually, I stopped going to her for help. I learned to shut out the voices and the shadows.

Sometimes, I don't even realize it's them anymore. The last time it happened, we were at a local battlefield, and I smelled the sweet, familiar scent of pipe tobacco, the kind my great-uncle used to smoke while I sat at the foot of his recliner watching old, animated movies. I thought it must've been from another visitor, but when I mentioned it, no one else could smell it.

Later, when I looked at the photos from that day, I saw the outline of a man in a uniform, holding a pipe, standing next to where I had been. I could see faces in the rocks around me.

I tried to show my husband, but he shook his head. "It's just shadows and a play of light," he said. I joked that his color blindness should help him see them better and that he needs better glasses.

But my mother believed me. She assured me that my experience was real, and shared similar experiences of her own.

Maybe that's why I don't have Grandmother's intensity. She leaned into her feelings, unafraid, while I've always pushed mine away. Grandmother said belief gives power to prayers and words. But I don't know if I can believe.

Sipping from my warm "Author" mug, I turn back to Elspet's story, trying to get back to where I left off.

CHAPTER NINE

THE STORY OF ELSPET BRUCE

Kisses not kept

Her prayers had been answered after weeks of waiting and the cold rain began pouring from the dark grey sky. As the wind grew, it pelted the hard stones of the house with loud thuds. Her father was busy going over the lecture for Sunday service and her mother sat tight-lipped by the fire, busying herself and Mary with patching the clothes and linens of some of the people in town for extra coin. Elspet quietly slipped out and slinked like a cat to the barn where she knew Tomas would be waiting.

Quietly, she opened the barn door, just enough to slide in and let out the smell of hay and feed. Closing the door, she felt as though lightning had struck deep inside her body as the firm grasp of her lover's hands planted around her waist. Her breath caught as she turned around. Her face and chest hurt from the joy and desire bursting within her. He kissed her immediately, and her lips pushed back against his with a violence unbecoming of a young woman. A quick flick of his tongue set something deep inside her aflame with a delicious fire.

She allowed him to guide her away from the door and toward an empty stall. Pieces of stray, pale yellow straw poked Elspet in an uncomfortable way as Tomas gently laid her down and began pulling her dress up. Grabbing his hands, she placed them on her shift, pulling them up together. The wait was too much, and she whimpered in need, grabbing at his breeches and pulling them down. She didn't have to wait long for the sinful promise to be fulfilled. Cupping his buttocks with both hands, she greedily drew him closer to her. He kissed the hollow of her neck and nibbled on her ears. She was as wet as the rain pounding outside as she continued to take him in deeper. He whispered that he loved her, that she would be his wife. The fire Tomas created in her was one that she would willingly burn all eternity for. They spoke in the language of lovers, certain the rain would mute their passion and provide them cover.

They were wrong though, for in their passion and rush, they failed to notice the old drunk woman asleep in the straw in the corner of the barn. Helen, a woman of ill manner, more often in her cups than out, had stumbled into the barn earlier to escape the rain and had fallen asleep. Their act woke her from her drunken slumber. She sat in a pile of old dirty straw, her greasy, grey-streaked hair falling in her face, giggling at the show before her. Jeering at them in a lewd manner. In a panic, Elspet pushed Tomas off her, yanking her dress down. Alarmed now too, Tomas stood up, pulling himself together.

"Tomas," Elspet said in a shrill squeak.

This will end them both. The law forbids carnal knowledge outside of marriage. A fine that Tomas cannot pay will mean prison and the pillory for him, and a whipping—or worse— for Elspet. Shame upon her and her family. The daughter of the Protestant priest being caught would only worsen the tensions in her village. In this country, the different factions had spilled so much blood already.

"We have to leave, now!" she cried, grabbing his hand and pulling it.

Tomas did not move with her, but instead toward Helen standing tall and broad-chested, squaring his shoulders over her, his fists in balls.

"Look at you Mistress Helen, in your cups again I see," Tomas said.

"Aye, and I see you were in Elspet's cups," she sneered with a laugh. The foul smell of old whisky and rot carried from her breath to the air around her.

"Unusual for you to be this far from town. Have you come to seek the good father for forgiveness of your sins?"

Helen tried to stand up, but stumbled, still drunk. "No, but maybe I should. There must be something to the dear father's sermons that I have been missing."

"You saw nothing, mistress, or should I say murderess?" Tomas threatened, pushing her back down into the straw as she tried to stand up once more.

"Aye, and they call me wicked," she said with a heavy sigh. "I saw nothing more than a couple of pigs rooting in the ground, nothing more." She gave a throaty laugh. As she walked unsteadily to the door, she called out, "Be careful, young ones, there is talk that the Devil is afoot in Forfar. I would hate to see you two be caught up in the Devil's work. He is everywhere in this country now, always has been."

CHAPTER
TEN

VOICES

"Nina?" I hear my mom's voice call out, sounding concerned. It startles me, pulling me out of the story I've been lost in.

"Mom?" I call back, but there's no response. Not even a bark from Cubby. I'm surprised—he usually barks and whines, jumping all over her for pets when she walks in. "Mom?" I call again, louder this time. Still nothing.

I push my desk chair back, only for the wheels to get stuck on a sweater I hadn't noticed falling off the back earlier. Frustrated, I shimmy out from between the chair and the desk, then hurry down the hallway, calling her name again as I head for the stairs.

The only response I get is from Cubby, who looks at me with a confused tilt of his head, then groans in annoyance for disturbing his nap. I continue down the stairs, but he follows me, staying underfoot and almost tripping me a few times, clearly demanding attention.

"Alright, alright, you win," I mutter, giving

in and letting him out into the yard.

As soon as the door opens, Cubby bounds out into the front yard, sniffing around for anything he might want to herd. His black-and-white coat shines in the sunlight. I take a moment to scan the driveway. No sign of Mom's car.

I know I heard her voice. It was clear and loud. Almost urgent. I'm sure of it.

"Cubby, come on," I call, bringing him back inside. I lock the door behind him and walk upstairs, trying to shake off the unease rising in my chest. I grab my phone and dial her number, just to make sure everything's okay.

Maybe I'm starting to get my grandmother's sixth sense, or maybe it's the part of my story I've been writing—the part with the Devil in it—that's messing with my head. The phone rings once, twice, before going to voicemail. I hang up, already knowing she never listens to her voicemails anyway, and try to calm myself down.

"It's going to be okay. She's fine," I mutter

under my breath. But the tightness in my chest doesn't ease.

I glance at my phone again. Six minutes. No response. I send a quick text: "Everything ok?" and sit back down at my desk, trying to refocus on my story. But my thoughts keep drifting back to my mom. Why hasn't she answered? Why did her voice sound so . . . off?

I check my phone again. No new messages. I'm starting to feel a prickling sensation at the back of my neck, telling me that something's wrong.

I call my grandmother. Thankfully, she picks up after two rings.

Her voice is tired, almost groggy. "Hello?"

"Hey, Grandma. Is Mom okay? Where is she?"

"Oh, she ran out to the store," she replies, but I hear the shift in her tone, the quiet worry creeping in. "She should be back soon."

I can tell I've made her nervous. The unease in her voice mirrors mine.

I hang up and let five more minutes slip by, then try calling Mom again. It rings, and rings. Still no answer.

Chewing on the inside of my lip, I try to focus back on my story. The words don't come as easily now. I keep looking at my phone, waiting for it to buzz with a message. I check the time again. Nine minutes since I sent the text.

The Devil certainly seems to have been in Forfar. But I don't believe it came from the accused witches, not all of them at least. Tomas threatens Helen, and then what?

I take a large sip from my tea, now cold. Looking down, I see a few tiny black specks of tea leaves floating around in the liquid. I swirl the cup absentmindedly, watching as they spin in a small whirlpool. I wish the leaves could tell me what happens next.

I take another sip and toy with the idea of reading the leaves. Why not? I place the cup down, close the document for my story, and pull up a search bar. *How to read tea leaves.*

I'm met with a surprising number of results. There are guides on the best teas to use, their spiritual properties, and how they can help with everything from deep sleep to lucid dreaming. I skim through the instructions:

"Place a pinch of loose tea leaves in a cup. Pour boiling water over them. Let steep, then drink most of the tea. When only a small amount is left, swirl the cup three times from left to right, then empty the remaining leaves onto a napkin."

I glance at my cup. The leaves inside look like coffee grounds. When dumped out, they just look like a messy pile of dirt. Hardly any fortune there.

Still, I'm curious. Grandma always said nothing works in the world without belief. And I do believe in the curse. I believe there's a connection between me and Elspet Bruce beyond just our blood. I just need a way to make our connection stronger, to be able to hear her better.

"Talk to me, Elspet," I whisper.

Suddenly, Cubby barks, loud and insistent.

Then the front door swings open and slams shut, making me jump out of my seat.

Chapter Eleven

Old Oven Mittens

"Hello?"

No one answers.

I get up from my desk, walking down the hallway. Peering at the bottom of the stairs, I see the front door wide open, the keys still hanging from the doorknob. My mother is crouched down, petting Cubby, who squeals like a pig in delight.

"Oh God, you scared me!" I place a hand over my heart.

My mom's light laugh rings through the house, easing some of the tension.

"What are you doing? I called but you didn't answer!" she says, feigning anger.

"I was just working on my story," I reply, pulling out my phone to check. "That's weird, I don't have a missed call. I called you."

"I know," she says, rolling her eyes, standing up and placing her purse on the coat hook by the door. "Between you and your grandmother, I had a ton of missed calls. I was at the store and didn't hear my phone ring. Sorry!"

"Are you working on your story about Elspet Bruce?" she asks, smiling. "I actually have more information about the Forfar witch trials if you want to hear."

She takes off her worn plastic slip-on shoes and follows me upstairs to my office.

"What's that?" she asks, pointing at the small pile of ground tea leaves on my desk.

"Oh, I was trying tea leaf reading for inspiration," I explain.

"I don't think that's the right kind of tea," she says, laughing.

"Oh, and what do you know about it?" I raise an eyebrow.

"Enough to know that it's probably not going to work with your grocery store brand of bagged tea." She shrugs, her expression suddenly serious. "Also, be careful with that stuff. You don't want to invite anything in."

She shifts her eyes around, like something's hiding in the shadows, ready to get us.

I can't help but laugh at her warning. She's

both religious and superstitious, and she regularly checks her horoscope. I've heard since I was little that every time we find a dime, it's from our family "ghost", who she believes is a male ancestor still watching out for us.

"I won't," I say, smiling. "So, what else did you find out about the witch trials?"

"I haven't had my coffee yet, and I'm getting a headache. Let's make some tea."

She gets up and heads downstairs. I follow her, putting the iron kettle back on the stove, and we wait for it to boil.

"You know, I have an electric kettle," she says, "and it heats water in like a minute. You should really get one."

"I like my kettle," I reply.

"Okay, Grandma," she teases.

"How's Grandma Anne doing, anyway?" I ask as we wait. I haven't seen her since their visit a few months ago. I know I should bring the kids by to visit soon, but I haven't mustered the energy to go.

"It's good days and bad," she says, her tone quieting. "Today's an okay day. She thinks she's me and I'm you. I just go along with it."

"That's probably best," I say softly.

"That's what the doctor says," she agrees. "She misses you, you know?"

"Probably because she can't remember that she doesn't like me," I joke.

"Probably," Mom laughs. "Anyway—the witch trials. Witch-hunting was basically the thing to do back then if you were a man in power. There was so much religious conflict between Catholics and Protestants at the time. About a hundred years before the witch trials, Queen Mary was burning Protestant reformers. If they'd kill you for being a Christian but not a Catholic, it wasn't much of a stretch to burn anyone else who didn't conform to the beliefs of those in charge. Throughout history, men in power have often directed public anger toward specific scapegoats to maintain control. 'Don't blame me for your crops failing and your children starving while I eat like a king, clearly, it's that poor old woman's fault!'"

"That's awful," I murmur.

"History isn't always pretty," she replies. "The first woman accused in Forfar was a poor woman named Isobel. Apparently, they were trying to take her property over a debt, and she cursed the man who came to collect."

"I'd probably curse him too," I say.

I hear the kettle begin to roll. I slip on my old oven mitt and pour the boiling water into our cups with aged Earl Grey tea bags. I grab the milk from the fridge for Mom's cup.

"I know, right?" Mom continues. "Basically, if you were a widowed or destitute woman, you were an easy target. One woman, Helen Guthrie, just went with it and started accusing everyone. Around fifty people were accused, and twenty-two were executed. Some of the women who managed to escape with their lives from the tollbooth were Elspet, her sister Mary and Helen's young daughter, Jane."

I seize on the mention of her name. "Anything more about Elspet?"

"Uh, rude," Mom says with a grin. "But no, not much. She was young and pretty, and she was accused of causing the death of some lady."

"Is she directly related to us?" I ask, taking a sip of the hot tea.

"I can't find a direct link," she answers, "but an offshoot branch definitely connects somewhere. Probably from the 'wrong side of the blanket,' as Grandma likes to say."

"Hmmm. Guess I'll have to resort to asking Elspet herself."

Mom laughs. "I guess so."

We sit in silence for a while, sipping our tea. Then my mother looks at me with a hint of concern in her eyes, tapping her fingers on her cup.

"Seriously, though, be careful with all that stuff. I know it seems harmless, but it's not always so. I remember when I was thirteen, my friends and I played with a Ouija board, thinking it was just a game. It freaked me out, and after that, I kept seeing a man with a beard in the mirror for years. Scared the crap out of me."

"It's only real if you believe it," I say, shrugging.

She gives me a stern look.

"I know that stuff is real. I promise I won't mess with Ouija boards or anything like that," I tell her. I won't. Those boards freak me out too. If God exists, then so does the Devil.

We sit quietly for a moment, lost in our own thoughts, before the sound of wind chimes from my mother's phone breaks the silence. She makes a face and answers.

"Yes, Mother. No, not yet. I'll give it to her now. Hold on, I'll put you on speaker."

"Hello?" Grandma's voice crackles through the speaker.

"Hi, Grandmother," I say.

"Hi, sweetie, do you like the gift?" she asks.

"Hold on," Mom interrupts. "I haven't given it to her yet. Just a second, please." She turns to dig in her purse.

"Oh, okay. Sorry," Grandma says.

I pull on a strand of hair, waiting.

When Mom turns back around, she's holding the iron cross in the palm of her open hand. There's a sharp pain as the hair I was pulling releases from my scalp, and I quickly close my fingers around it, forcing a smile.

"Oh, are you sure you want to give this away?" I ask.

"I'm getting old, honey," Grandmother says, her voice trembling through the phone. "My mother didn't pass it on to me before she left, and I don't want that to be how you receive it, from a stranger instead of from me."

I glance at Mom, searching for help, but she just smiles and hands me the cross.

"Thank you," I say, my voice thick.

"Is she smiling? Does she love it?" Grandma asks eagerly.

"Yes, and she can hear you. You're on speaker," Mom responds.

"Oh, okay. I love you, sweetie. I know I don't say it enough, but I do."

"I love you too, Grandma," I say.

Mom ends the call, leans over, and wraps me in a big hug, whispering, "Thank you."

She takes the cross necklace from my hand and places it around my neck, adjusting it before standing up to take a photo for Grandma. Once she's done, I stand and give her a hug in return.

"Thank you. And who knows? Maybe Elspet is the ancestor the cross came from."

"Maybe," I say, sitting back down.

"I need to get back to your grandmother, but I've found all I can about the Forfar trials and Elspet. When it comes to your story, I think it's time to trust your creativity and instincts," Mom says.

"Thanks. I'll just ask God and the ancestors for inspiration next," I reply, grinning.

"I'm glad you found a hobby, though. Something to channel your energy into in a healthy way," she says, reaching out to touch the cross hanging from my neck. "Just be careful which ancestors you call. Not all of them are winners."

"They've never listened to me before, and they probably won't now," I mumble. "Not unless I believe in my ability to do so."

"What was that?"

"Just something Grandma told me once, that power comes from belief," I say.

Mom walks over and wraps her hand around the side of my head, pushing it gently into her stomach, then places a kiss on top of my head.

"Be careful what you believe in," she says softly, her gaze lingering on me for a moment before she heads toward the door. She stops, turning back to me. "And be careful what you don't."

The cross weighs heavily against my collarbone as I watch her walk out the door, my ancestors now pressing heavily on my mind and spirit

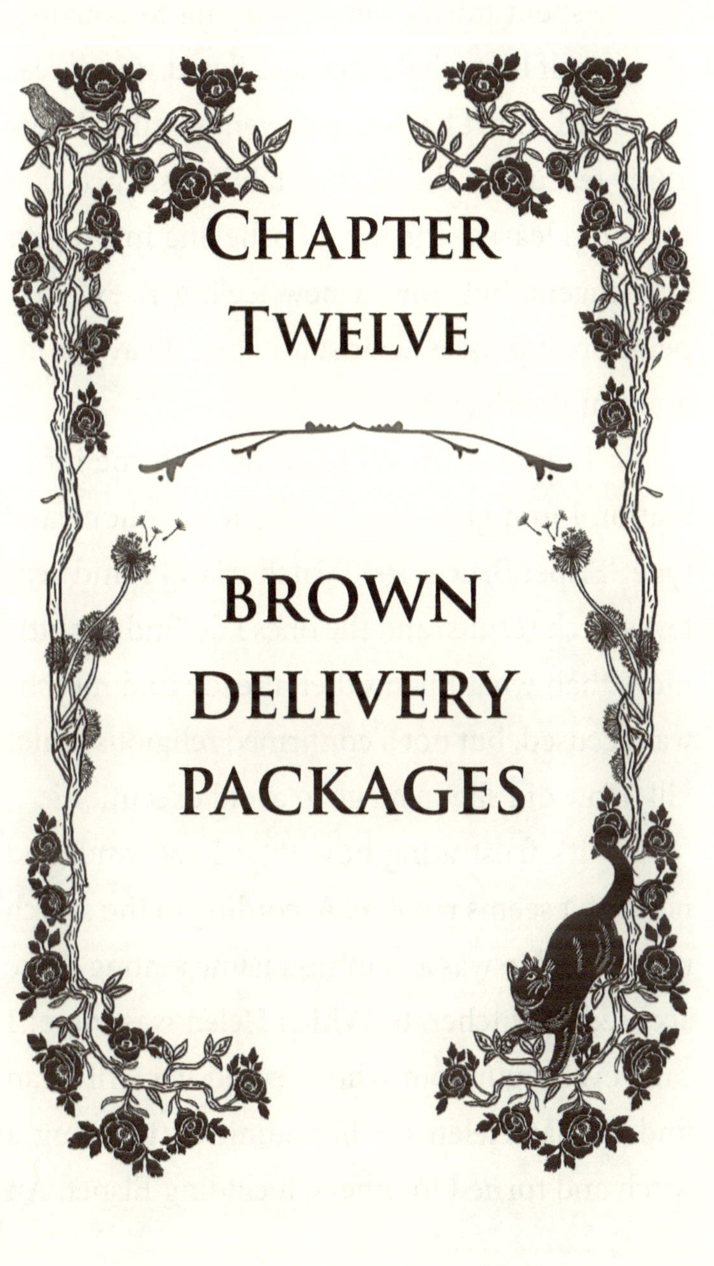

Chapter Twelve

Brown Delivery Packages

I've spent most of my life trying to convince myself that what I saw and heard wasn't real, that I didn't have any power, no gifts. I stare at my teacup on the kitchen table in silence after my mom leaves. The fear of believing in my gifts still lingers, but now, a new feeling rises—desperation. It presses against my chest, heavy as my grandmother's cross.

There isn't much to go on with the information Mom gave me. I pull out my phone and type "Elspet Bruce, 1600 witch trials." I find very few search results, and the ones I do find say little more than what my mother already told me: she was accused, but not a confirmed religious zealot kill. How did she manage to avoid execution?

It's frustrating how little I can find, and none of it seems reliable. According to the search results, Helen was a common name among those accused of witchcraft. Which Helen was mine? I can't even figure out who accused her. All I can find is that Helen readily admitted to being a witch and turned in others, including Elspet. An icy feeling crawls over me every time I read her name. There's no doubt in my mind that Helen was terrible; she seems to have had a nasty reputation before ever being accused of a witch. According to some books on the Scottish witch trials, she even killed her sister before the trials started. She accused so many innocent people of witchcraft. Was it out of fun? Revenge? Was she a woman who sacrificed others to prolong her daughter's life? Was she simply evil, or—was she really a witch?

Maybe Elspet was just the innocent victim of a curse put on her by Helen, and maybe that curse has followed us through the generations.

As I continue to dig into the Forfar witch trials, my phone begins to populate with ads for books on other trials, then books on witches and spells. One catches my eye: *Celtic Spells and Scottish Ancestry*. I place the order, and soon my feed is flooded with similar suggestions, tarot cards, dowsing rods, candles, and a Bruce tartan scarf. I might as well go all in, right? What's the worst that could happen? Attract more bad luck? We're already cursed, and now I wear the cross necklace.

I grab a strand of hair and rub the end back and forth over my mouth, searching for one last item: mugwort tea. I've always had strong dreams, vivid dreams, both good and bad. Sometimes my dreams even have their own soundtrack. But the nightmares have always left me shaken for days. Often times, the nightmares are of me being trapped by shadows, unable to escape, unable to control anything. Lucid dreaming—being able to control the dream—might be my best shot at understanding what happened with Elspet and the family curse. If I can have some sort of control in my dreams, I can see beyond the shadows and get some answers.

I hover my mouse over the order button, and a wave of unease starts to build in my stomach, rising up and threatening to choke me. I shake my head, move the mouse to select next-day shipping, and click order. It's for research purposes, I tell myself. I feel uneasy, though, and the sense of shadows lurking just beyond my sight only grows. I try to shake off the fear that's been riding shotgun in my life for as long as I can remember.

I go back to searching for ways to connect with ancestors, but everything I find involves spells. I'm not comfortable with that. I believe my mother's warning about being careful with what, and who, I call to. While I want to learn more about what happened at Forfar, I don't want to risk making the curse worse.

Grandmother always warned us that Ouija boards and tarot cards were for those seeking to use gifts they didn't naturally possess. That they only worked because of the power given by something else, not by God. I wonder if I'm making a mistake with my purchases.

Elspet, please send me a sign that I'm on the right path.

I touch the cross. Maybe Mom was right. Maybe this is my link to her.

With a sigh, I stand, grab my teacup, and head toward the door. Something shiny on the floor catches my eye. It is a dime, and I smile.

Chapter Thirteen

Tied Up with Strings

It hasn't happened in years, not since I was a teenager. That fear, the realization that I can't move. I can see, I can hear, but my body won't obey. Frozen, paralyzed, while everything around me continues as if nothing is wrong. I can feel the warmth of my husband's body next to mine. I can hear the occasional whine from Cubby at the foot of our bed as he dreams, the stirring of my children in their beds down the hall. Panic sets in. My heart beats like the wings of a frightened bird against the bars of a cage, frantic to escape.

I beg my body to move, just a finger to twitch, a toe to wiggle, but it's like my body is made of cement, glued to the bed. My body is a prison, and I'm desperately trying to break free.

I catch glimpses of shadows moving across the walls, seen only from the corner of my eyes. The terror they bring is more than I can bear. I want to scream, to cry out for help, but my voice is trapped in silence.

Please, God, I beg in my mind. *Please protect me. Please forgive me.*

What feels like a hand presses into the small of my back. I want to shake it off, to leap up and run, or face the shadows head-on, but my body is bound, my cheek stuck to the pillow.

The iron cross around my neck begins to burn where it touches the skin of my collarbone. It feels like my spirit is vibrating, trying to leave. *Please*, I beg my body. *Please move. Please, I will fight this. I will not let this take me.*

It feels as though my body, my soul, is about to be overtaken. I push back against the weight of it, shouting silently to the walls of my mind that I will not sell my soul, I will not be possessed.

Then I feel it, a light brush of fingers, or perhaps lips, against my right ear. My entire body buzzes with a strange, electric energy.

God, please save me!

This is the first sensation I can feel. I focus on it, pushing into the tingling, pins-and-needles sensation that spreads across my skin. Slowly, agonizingly, I manage to move my finger. Then my hand. The spell is broken. I can move again.

My heart thuds in my chest as I quickly scan the room, frantic. I get up and rush to my children's room, checking that they are still breathing, still safe. When I return to bed, I curl as close to my husband as I can, seeking his warmth, his protection.

But it doesn't take long for the pins-and-needles sensation to return, creeping back, making my skin prickle. I glance up and see a shadow, that of a woman in a hood, moving toward me. Panic floods through me. I sit up, gasping, and the shadow recedes. The burning on my collarbone fades. I lay back down, my heart still racing, and I pull my husband's arm around me, holding on as if I could keep whatever is lurking at bay.

Too afraid to let myself slip into sleep again, I wait. My heartbeat slows, but my mind is still reeling. After a while, I slide out of bed, unable to rest. The clock reads 3:00 AM. I have to be up in three hours anyway.

I go downstairs, needing the comfort of a cup of tea, trying to remind my body that we're not in fight-or-flight mode. As I pass the vanity, I pause and reach for the clasp of the iron cross necklace, intent on taking it off. But my fingers hesitate. They linger on the clasp, then drop to the cross itself, as if waiting for something I can't name.

After a moment, I let my hands fall to my sides and stare at my reflection in the dark mirror. I look like a shadow version of myself, hair wild and unkempt from lack of sleep, face drawn with exhaustion.

I turn away from the mirror and leave my room. As I head downstairs, I grab my laptop from the office. If I can't sleep, at least I can write.

Chapter Fourteen

The Story of Elspet Bruce

Debts owed

I have not seen Tomas since Mistress Helen caught us in the barn fifteen days ago. Tomas said not to worry, that no one would believe a woman such as her. One so often in her cups and covered in filth. If that were true, then I do not see why he would threaten her so forcefully, and it does little to ease my fear. There is something changing in our town, like the hidden depths of a treacherous stream that I fear I am unable to navigate. Once friendly faces are now cold, rigid, and full of suspicion. The little bowls of milk and bits of bread left for the small folk are steadily disappearing from the doors and windowsills of the houses I pass when running errands for Mother. Something has changed in Tomas since that day as well. He was rough with Mistress Helen, and two days of rain have passed without him coming to meet me. My heart fills with both fear and despair.

Minister Robertson has been speaking about the evils lurking in other towns across Scotland and England. They say there is a plague of witches, and that they are prepared in case such evil should arrive here in Forfar. There is a sense of unease throughout the village, and I have been avoiding it. Taking care to tend to the animals, collecting and delivering eggs from the chickens, and enjoying a reprieve from Mother's watchful eye as she has been preoccupied with other things of late. Mistress Isobel has been having a rough go of it since her husband passed last winter. Despite not having much ourselves, Father has encouraged me to drop off some eggs to help get her through the grief of losing her husband and, with that, her main source of income. Father often asks that we give whatever we can spare to help others, much to the annoyance of Mother.

I wish it was to Aunt Agnes he would send me. The path to her house at this time of year is beginning to thicken with the comforting smells of wild herbs and flowers. She is always happy to show me what plants she is drying and what their uses are.

The trudge through the thick, early morning

fog that comes off the marshes makes the prospect of a visit to Mistress Isobel that much more unwelcoming. Despite her recent loss, I do not like her much. She has taken to drinking along with some of the other women in town, especially Mistress Helen. Her demeanor has changed much since her husband died, her once friendly smile is quite often a scowl.

As I come upon her house, I hear her shrieking break through the gentle rustling of the trees. I drop the basket of eggs, feeling some of them break under my feet as I run, afraid that something must be wrong, and she is in need of help. As I get closer, I can see from behind her spring house that she is yelling at a man. It is George, one of the town officials.

"Your taxes are past due, mistress, you need to settle the full account or forfeit your property," he says firmly.

"How dare you come to my home and threaten to take my land. This home has been in my husband's family for generations."

"Don't be angry at me, mistress, it is your husband's fault he did not leave you with a means to cover his debts. You should consider remarrying, or perhaps seek out relatives who may take pity on you." George walks over and hands her a paper.

Ripping the paper from his hand and tearing it in half, Mistress Isobel throws it back at George.

"I will give you a week to get your affairs in order and leave," he says, walking away red-faced. No sooner does he reach his horse that she points her finger at him.

"You want to take my land so badly, then you shall have it. I curse your name and bid you to never step foot off it again!"

The leaves in the nearby trees stop rustling, then the only sound in the air is George gasping for breath. The portly man clutches his chest and falls.

I cover my mouth to stifle the scream that threatens to break free and betray my presence. The silence is broken by the loud cackling of

Mistress Isobel, who is soon joined by a chorus of birds. It is a frightful sound, and I run as far as I can from that place. The wind begins to blow, causing the trees to creak in a manner that sounds as if the very gates of Hell are opening around me. I run fast, faster than I have ever run, afraid the trees will scoop me up in their branches. By the time I reach home, my chest feels as though it will burst. I don't even notice Master Alfred until I run into him so hard that I bounce back and onto the ground in front of the door.

"Elspet?" he says in shock, picking me up, but I push past him and into the house, startling my mother who is washing up in a basin by the fireplace.

"Elspet?" she questions, but I push past her to mine and Mary's room, shaking my head as she calls out again, "Elspet, what did you see?"

I dare not tell her what I witnessed. I know in my heart that darkness is not coming; it is already here, and Forfar will never be the same again.

Chapter Fifteen

Black Horses and Carriages

The sound of heavy footsteps descending the staircase and a cry of "Momma!" yank me out of the world of Elspet and back into reality. I hit Save five times on my document before closing my laptop and getting up from the table to greet my children with big hugs, followed by a chorus of "Good mornings" and "I missed yous."

The morning slips away much too quickly, as it always does. Breakfast is made, lunches and water bottles are packed. Arguments over socks and hair are followed by ten more minutes of morning cartoons before I have to shut them off, leading to cries and bribes of morning candy if they get into the car without a fuss.

My daughter tries to dash out the door after her father, but I grab her hand, holding her back with me. Unhappy with being tethered, she twists out of my grip and takes off toward the giant tree near where my husband stands, its storm-battered, broken branches from a windstorm months ago are looming overhead. I yell for my husband to stop her; he doesn't see what I do. The branches, damaged in the last storm, stretch out, waiting to fall. I can already imagine one breaking free, falling at just the right moment and angle, landing squarely on her head or pinning her to the ground.

I take off running after her but miss a step from the entryway and fall hard. Pain shoots up from my palms and knees. My right ankle feels as though it's on fire. Panic surges as I scramble to get up, my eyes darting to my daughter, still running toward the tree.

"What the hell just happened?" my husband yells, rushing toward me. "Can you walk?"

"Get the kids!" I screech, trying to stand and get them myself, but the pain of putting weight on my ankle is unbearable. I sit back down, scooting myself toward the door, dragging my bleeding palms across the floor.

The kids come running up behind my husband, and they soon all surround me. I pull my son and daughter both in for a hug, comforting myself as much as them.

"I'm fine," I assure him and the kids, breathless. "Just take the kids to school."

He hesitates, clearly torn, but both kids are upset, and he's already late for work.

"Just go," I repeat, trying to reassure him, and give the kids one last hug before he leads them to the car.

"Stay away from that tree!" I shout as they pass it, my heart still pounding.

Though my ankle throbs and my hands and knees are bleeding, I'm relieved it was me who was injured and not my daughter. Once they are safely in the car, I continue to make my way inside the house. I sit on the bottom step of the staircase behind our entryway, pushing away the negative thoughts that begin to creep in. Why does this always happen to me?

It isn't long before my phone rings. It's my husband.

"Hey, are the kids okay?" I ask, trying to keep my voice steady.

"Yeah, they're fine. Are you okay?" he asks.

"What the hell was that? Why are you afraid of Audrey running in the yard? I had her. She wasn't going anywhere near the street. It's not like we live next to a highway."

"No, I know that," I reply, frustration bubbling up. "It's the branches on the tree. The ones that got damaged in the storm. They were dangling above her, and if one of them fell—"

"Are you serious? The branches are fine," he interrupts, his tone flat. "I'll take another look when I get home, but if you're that worried about it, I'll call someone to trim the trees."

I can hear the annoyance in his voice, and it stings. He doesn't understand my fears, the thoughts that never leave my mind. I've always felt like I have to be hyper-vigilant because I know most people don't see the dangers I do. They don't prepare, they don't plan for the worst. But I do. Every possible outcome, every conversation, every step is already mapped out in my head. People who've never experienced something bad happening don't understand. They can't.

I don't fault them for it. I don't even envy their ignorance anymore. I pity them. They won't be ready when something does happen. And in my family, something always does.

Years ago, before I had children, I was in a car accident commuting to work. It was just me in the car, thankfully. I was rear-ended, my car totaled, my nose broken, and I had a bad concussion. I remember looking in my rearview mirror, seeing the woman behind me speeding up as I was slowing down to stop. I remember thinking: *She has to stop. She has to.*

I remember the panic coursing cold through my veins as I tried to move my car to the side of the road, but I was blocked by construction barriers. The first impact jolted me forward. The second pushed me into the car in front of me by inches. I had left plenty of space, prepared for something like this. But I was still hit.

It's been years, but every time I see a car speeding up behind me in my rearview, that panic still grips me. The migraines are still there.

And my nose . . . it's a little less straight than it was.

It doesn't take long for my husband to return home. He insists we go to the walk-in clinic to get checked out. I try to argue that there's no need. I have a boot and crutches in the closet from previous falls, plus some 800mg pain relievers. But he doesn't listen and lifts me into his arms, carrying me to the car despite my protests.

After hours of waiting, the X-ray confirms there's nothing broken, just a bad sprain. There's nothing to do but rest, ice, and elevate.

The drive home is quiet. I reach for his hand in the car, and he doesn't pull away when I place mine on top of his.

When we pull into the driveway, I glance up at the branches of the tree. They don't look as threatening now, but I can still see the danger.

My husband helps me out of the car and into the house, setting me up on the couch with my laptop, snacks, and water. He's nothing like my father, who was only a slightly better version of my grandfather. While our women may still be cursed, at least our taste in men has improved. He places my old crutches beside me and gives me a quick kiss before heading out for work.

I text my boss to let them know what happened, and instead of working, I take my pain relievers and begin searching again for anything related to Elspet Bruce in the 1700s.

I look through various genealogy sites, but nothing turns up that my mother hasn't already found. None of my searches on what happened to Elspet after the witch trials yield any new information, either. The only difference I can find is that she was one of three women, not two, who survived the trials. A slight change from what we'd previously found.

Annoyed, I put my phone down and pick up the book of Celtic spells I'd ordered. I thumb through it until I find what I'm looking for: a summoning spell.

Grandmother always warned us about using tools to contact the dead. She said it was unnatural, that if we were meant to receive something, it would come to us.

But I know I need help. I need Elspet. I need to break this cycle, this curse, before the next injury is my daughter's instead of mine. I can't let fear hold me back anymore, not when my children's safety and well-being depend on it.

The book instructs me to create a meaningful space, something to welcome the ancestor. I hesitate, not daring to take off the necklace, fearing that my daughter might find it if I do. Instead, I pick up the tartan scarf I purchased and set aside a space in my office.

Once I'm done, I return to my desk and pull out the bottle of pain reliever I have stashed in the drawer. Hoping to ease the pain in my ankle or at least dull it enough to not be a distraction. I open my laptop and resume writing after swallowing the medicine. Grasping the cross, I whisper, "Show me, Elspet."

I conjure her image in my mind, her dark auburn hair falling down her back, and focus on the memories of my ancestors. The smells, sounds, and scents of Scotland, where our line came from. I keep calling out to Elspet in my thoughts, and then, I begin to write.

CHAPTER SIXTEEN

THE STORY OF ELSPET BRUCE

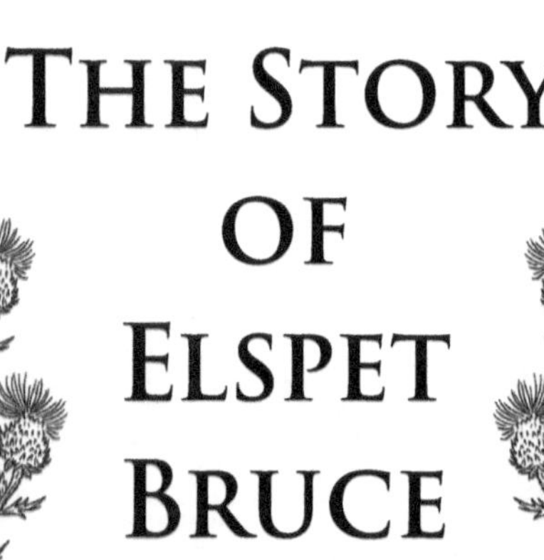

Spells and lies

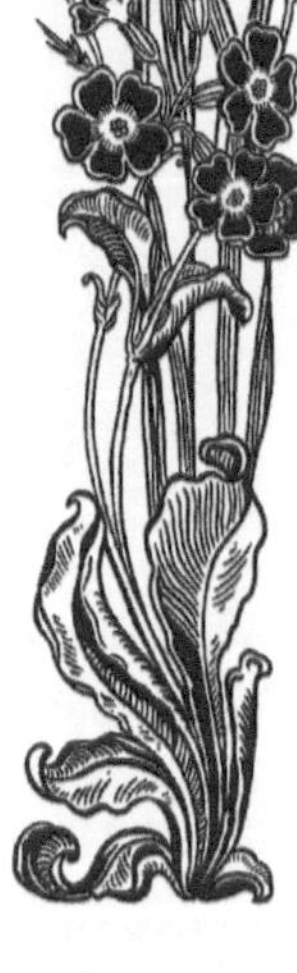

I haven't thought about it, I didn't keep track of the time. Not until my mother mentioned gathering moss and wool in preparation for our bleeding. I haven't seen Tomas in weeks, and I have missed my bleeding and begun to feel unwell. It is not the first time I have gone to my aunt for help, to her cottage outside of town. She has tea that will bring on your courses, ensuring you will not be with child if you take it early enough. I wait until my mother leaves to visit a friend, but before she walks out of the door, she hands me a note.

"Elspet, I need you to visit my sister and hand her this letter. I am not feeling well, and I need her to make something for me."

"Are you unwell, Mother?" I ask, though I am relieved that I do not have to sneak off to see Aunt Agnes and am eager to accept the task.

"Never you mind, do as your told now," she says.

Taking the note from Mother, I walk as fast as I can. I reach her house within a few hours and knock, but she does not answer. I knock louder and call her name but still no answer. I go toward the back of Agnes's house where she keeps her garden and see her there, kneeling in the soil and caring for the earth and plants as if they were her dear children, singing to them an old song unfamiliar to me. Her dark hair is streaked with grey and wisdom.

"What is it?" she asks gruffly when she sees me.

"Auntie, I have a note from my mother, she is not feeling well."

"Again?"

Again? What does she mean again? Getting up slowly, she walks toward me, smacking her hands against one another to shake off the earth. She reaches a soiled hand out for the note, reads it quickly, and then tucks it into her apron pocket.

"Tell your mother I will pray for her," she says, turning back to her work and walking away.

"I also need something. The tea, Auntie," I say, standing firmly before her.

She walks back over to me slowly, her brow creasing and her lips tight. "You are your mother's daughter, and so I will pray for you too."

"I don't need your damn prayers," I say, panic setting in.

"My dear child, it is my prayers, and the prayers of the women before me that keep you safe. You need them more than you know."

"If you don't help me, I will make it myself." I push my way past her into her garden but am stopped by her strong grasp on my arm.

"With which knowledge will you be making it then?"

I say nothing, keeping my fists locked and gazing toward her garden.

"Surely not your own as you've yet to demonstrate that you have any. More often lost in a daydream than you are committing to memory the knowledge I've tried to pass down to you." I feel her presence wrap around me as she comes closer until I feel her lips hovering by my ear. Her hand rests on my shoulder. "There are whispers on the streets of witchcraft. If I give you this and they find out, I will be among the accused. If I let you make it yourself, you will likely die." She moves to stand before me now, her gaze not unkind, but concerned and conflicted.

"I promise, I won't tell anyone," I beg her, grabbing her arm in desperation.

She looks at me, her pity finally weighing out as she tells me to wait and walks back into her house. I follow quietly behind her, much to her annoyance. "You're far too pretty to have your skin scarred by the crack of the whip for having a child out of wedlock, though maybe it would teach you a lesson about who you let into your quey. I do believe it would be far worse for your dear father, the sweet man, to have his own daughter punished so harshly. I reckon it would be far worse for my own heart as well." I stand quietly in front of her, eyes cast down and hands grasped in front of me. I can feel her eyes on me, as though she is peering into my soul before finally breaking the silence.

"Come inside my house, I suspect it will not be long before they come for me too. They've turned their back on the old ways, claim it to not be of God and his work. God created us in his image. The plants, the animals, and the earth are as close to him as we can get. Men have been looking for reasons to dispose of us once we are no longer useful, our faces no longer fair, our bodies no longer fit for pleasure or work or for bearing children that they themselves take no responsibility for. I have only begun to teach you about the plants and herbs from my garden and the woods these past few years, but there is so much more to know. This knowledge should not die with me but be saved and passed down to others so they can heal in the old ways. It will be your turn one day to help others as I have helped you, and you should pray for them as I have done for you too."

I follow her into the house and close the door quietly. I sit in the old worn-out chair by the fireplace, from which bittersweet scent of the herbs hanging to dry reach me. I recognize the foxglove and dandelion bunches that hang. The herbs that I once saw as my freedom now begin to feel like a burden to be inherited. She sits down next to me with a cup of hot tea.

"Here, drink this now, but I'll not give it to you again. This is a dangerous game you play, one that can end your life if you continue. I know this, because I have watched it end others who have used it. I tell you this, so you can understand the sacrifices that were made for the knowledge of healing, of using these plants given to us by God. The consequences of misusing this knowledge, of not respecting it."

"I understand Auntie," I say.

The tea gives off a familiar and comforting smell of spearmint, and the hot liquid burns as it goes down. Aunt Agnes watches me for a moment, seeming deep in thought. Her hand gently tugging on the cross necklace that usually lay tucked within the top of her dress.

"I heard they came for Mistress Isobel's

land now that her husband has gone to the Lord. I suspect they will come for me before too long. It's already been many summers since your dear uncle passed. Are you ready Elspet? Can you handle the responsibility that comes with knowledge, that comes with a gift?"

Handing the empty cup back to her I say, "I am, Auntie."

Aunt Agnes has already taught me a lot about plants and herbs that can be used for healing, but it's mostly been for minor things—tea's for settling stomachs, salves for soothing rashes. I know now that she will be teaching me medicines to save lives, as she has saved my life with this tea. I know some consider this witchcraft. That they move further away from the knowledge of our ancestors and toward the ignorance of the kings in charge. But making teas and medicines from the plants God has given us is no more witchcraft than making stews for dinner using the same plants and animals God put on this earth for us.

After spending hours at her house, learning how to make the very tea I had come there for, she packs the leaves into a small cloth satchel and tells me to give it to my mother.

"My mother? Why would she need this?"

Aunt Agnes looks at me thoughtfully and says, "The world is often as others want us to see it, and not as it is."

"What does that mean, Auntie?"

"This tea brings on your flux. For some women, such as yourself, it clears a seed not yet rooted. For others who are nearing the end of their season, they believe it can give them more time."

"More time?" I ask.

"Our worth is often tied to our season, you know this. When a woman's season ends, a new one begins, but it is of less value to some."

She shuts the door behind me and leaves me to walk home alone, contemplating her words and the medicine I carry.

As I pass through the main street of town,

I hear the rumbling of some kind of commotion. I hear calls of "Witch" and fear strikes me. Following the clamorous noise, I find a heaving crowd gathered at the tollbooth. They have taken Mistress Isobel. As the crowd jeers and pushes her toward the small prison, she does nothing but laugh and toss curses at them. Finally, she is forced into the tiny cell. The town governor addresses the crowd, saying what she stands accused of and asking if anyone has evidence of her witchery to step forward.

I see Tomas standing in the crowd and rush to his side.

"Tomas," I whisper. He glances at me briefly.

"Tomas," I say again, reaching for his arm. He brushes off my reach and pushes his way to the front of the crowd.

"I did witness Mistress Helen with Mistress Isobel together at the kirkyard three nights ago. A coldness came upon me at the sight of them singing and dancing naked in the moonlight.

There was a black cat standing upon its two feet like a demon, dancing along with them," Tomas yells out.

My stomach sinks and my blood runs cold at his lies.

A murmur ripples through the crowd and soon others begin to add accusations against the women such as bad luck, crop failures, or the illness, or death of livestock. Tomas turns toward me and we lock eyes. I feel as though I have been punched in the stomach. His face looks so different to me than when I last saw him. It is hardened and angry, and I fear for him and myself. I fear for our love.

The crowd stays, looking at the accused. Black horses pulling a black funeral carriage soon drive by, capturing Tomas's attention and freeing me from his eyes. The carriage carries the body of the man Mistress Isobel had cursed not yet a week ago. I push my way toward Tomas, grabbing his arm, but he pulls away, shaking his head. I want to cry but fight back the tears. I know I should speak up, but I can't, I am frozen in fear. My stomach cramps as the tea begins to work, and I turn to walk home, away from what I fear will ruin us all. Black clouds roll in and thunder booms ahead. It's hard not to think that this is the work of the Devil.

Chapter Seventeen

Dandelion Wishes

"Hey, Mom."

"Hey, I know your ankle's still bothering you, but do you think you could manage to drive by the house and check on your grandmother?"

"Yeah, I think I can handle that. I barely use crutches now that I have a boot. Is everything okay?" I ask, saving my work and closing the laptop.

"She hasn't answered her phone, which isn't exactly surprising, she forgets how to use the thing half the time," Mom replies, "but I can't see her on the cameras, and that's what worries me."

I pull up the app on my phone and check the four cameras we installed last year in the living room, kitchen, and her bedroom. There's no sign of her. The anxiety that had been simmering in my chest bubbles over, and a deep sense of dread tightens my throat.

"Yeah, I'll leave now. I'll call you when I get there," I say, my voice already tight with worry.

"Thank you. I owe you. I'm stuck at my

doctor's appointment and won't get home for a few hours. It was hard to get it, so I don't want to leave and risk waiting months for another one," my mom says, the frustration and concern clear in her voice.

"It's no problem," I assure her before hanging up. I grab my purse and keys, heading out the door.

As I drive the twenty minutes to her house, I dial my grandmother's number every five minutes. But each call goes unanswered. The panic in my chest tightens. Where is she? What could have happened? I need to concentrate on the road, but my mind is filling with horrible images of what I might find when I get there.

When I finally arrive, I knock on the door, but there's no answer. I punch in the code to the door lock, and the door swings open, the little dog my mother got my grandmother last year begins barking furiously as I step inside. The sound of running water reaches me.

"Grandmother?" I call out.

I follow the sound to the bathroom, the only place where the cameras don't have a view. When I enter the open door, I find her swaying in front of the sink, mumbling to herself. The mirror is fogged over with steam.

"Grandmother!" I shout, rushing to her side.

To my horror, I see her hands, red and raw, rubbing furiously under the scalding water.

"Grandma, stop!" I yank her wrists away, gasping as the hot water burns my hands. "Ow, fuck!"

But my grandmother just looks at me, dazed, then back down at her hands.

"The blood, it won't come off," she murmurs. "Look, there's blood on yours too. We must get it off."

"It's okay, Grandma, it's okay," I mutter, trying to stay calm. I turn off the faucet and gently guide her to sit on the toilet. Then I grab a hand towel and run it under cold water to wrap around her scalded hands.

"You're going to be okay," I reassure her, even though I'm shaking inside. She seems oblivious to the pain, her hands submerged in the towel.

I call my mom to update her on what's happening, but she doesn't pick up. I unwrap my grandmother's hands and see they're still bright red.

"The blood," she repeats softly.

"It's okay," I tell her gently. "You got it all off. It's gone now. But you did a little too good of a job. We need to go to the doctor."

"No. No, I'm not going," she protests weakly.

"We have to, Grandma," I say.

I coax her down the hallway, out the door, and into my car, then drive straight to the emergency room, heart pounding. Thank God they take her back immediately.

The doctors wrap her hands and confirm that she's suffered first and second-degree burns. But it's their questions that make my stomach churn. They feel like an interrogation.

"How long was she alone?" one nurse asks.

"How long was she washing her hands? What's the temperature on your hot water heater, and why don't you keep it set lower to prevent something like this?"

Another question: "Why isn't she in a care facility if you can't provide the proper care?"

Each one feels like a reprimand, and the guilt weighs heavier with every word.

Once the medical team and the social worker leave, I'm finally allowed to sit with my grandmother. It's just the two of us now.

"I'm sorry," I say, my voice small.

"For what?" she asks, confused.

"For not getting here sooner, and for your hands being burned," I whisper, the guilt still clawing at me.

"It's not your fault, sweetheart," she says, her voice soft but clear. "I wish I could remember what happened. I remember turning the sink on, but I don't remember the water being so hot."

I don't tell her what else she's forgotten, that she was trying to wash the blood off, convinced that she'd hurt someone. I don't want to upset her with that. For now, I just hold her wrists lightly, feeling where the bandages end beneath my fingers. She seems more lucid now, as if the fog has cleared for a moment despite the pain medication, and the grandmother I used to know is back. Tears start to spill from my eyes, and she notices.

"Nina, it's not your fault," she says gently. "I'm fine."

"I just feel bad," I choke out, wiping my cheeks. "This always happens to our family. It's like we can't ever catch a break. No matter what, something bad always happens."

"What are you doing?" she asks as I start to unhook the cross necklace from around my neck.

"I'm giving it back," I say, my voice thick. "You gave it to me, and then I end up here with you in the hospital. Maybe you're right, and it was protecting you."

"Oh, sweetie, no," she says, her eyes softening. "I want you to have it. Bad things happen to everyone, but we are blessed. I know it's hard to see, but it could be worse. We always make it out okay. Just like my mother and grandmother prayed for me, I pray for you. Your prayers will protect your own children and their children. All the prayers of the women in our line, they are still with us. That necklace isn't the only thing that carries those prayers. You do too. God never gives us more than we can handle. The pain is temporary. Don't worry about me. I'm going to be fine." She holds up her bandaged hands. "I'm the dummy who washed my hands in scalding water."

"I just feel like we're always being punished," I say again, my tears flowing freely.

"Pain lets you know you're alive." Her voice is calm and steady. "Grief lets you know you are loved and have loved."

After another hour at the hospital, my mom finally arrives to relieve me. I kiss my grandmother's forehead as she flirts with her doctors and nurses, her smile returning.

"I love you, honey," she says as I head out.

She tells me not to feel guilty, but guilt and fear, those are things I've lived with my whole life. I don't know how to live without them. It must be our inheritance from Elspet. I'm sure of it now. With every word I write about her, I feel our connection growing stronger. I wish we could have inherited something other than pain, trauma, and a curse.

I make it home and run through the usual nightly routine: dinner, playtime, and bedtime. But the guilt lingers, distracting me, making me feel less present for my husband and kids. My husband, as always, gives me grace. The kids sense my melancholy, offering hugs and picked flowers. I take their gifts with a smile, but I wish they would hurry up and go to sleep so that I can get back to my laptop.

Once they're asleep, I slip out of their rooms and head back to my office—to Elspet.

I think about her silence and mine, the choices she's made, and the choices I've made. It's funny how, in your head, you believe you'd always stand up for what's right. You think you'd have the courage to do the right thing, no matter the consequences. I'd like to think I would. So many people in history risked their lives for what was right. I want to believe I wouldn't be like the Elspet in my story now, the one who stayed silent, who didn't speak up when it mattered most.

But as I write her story, I wonder if I'd have had the courage as an adult. You never know until you're in that moment, facing that kind of evil. Maybe that makes me closer to her than I thought. The doubt that I would be able to do the right thing, the fear that I'd be too much of a coward.

It's hard to know when to speak up and when to stay silent. My grandmother always said she wished she had spoken up about the rumors of her father's affair, that maybe if she had, her mother would still be here. But it's hard to say.

It's unfair to put that kind of responsibility on a young person's shoulders. Sometimes, it doesn't matter what you do. The outcome is set in stone.

I hope my brother knew that I loved him before he died. He's gone because he was trying to keep me out of trouble. I was the one who pushed the wagon at the top of the hill. I should have told my mother what happened when he hit his head, but he told me not to. I should have ignored him. Maybe he'd still be alive if I had.

The computer screen flickers, and a pen falls to the floor. As I bend down to pick it up, the cross necklace taps me lightly on the nose. A dime rolls out from under the desk, and I smile softly, knowing some spirits are still with us, showing us signs that they're near. My mom and grandmother always say that. It's why they smile when they see a stray dime. It's why they get excited when a red cardinal swoops past the window. It's why I don't spray my lawn for weeds, and instead, I welcome the dandelions, the same ones my brother and I used to blow and make wishes on. Every dandelion puff reminds me of him, of the love we shared, and how he's still here, in the wind, in the memories, in the spirit of the dandelions.

When my grandmother closes her eyes for the last time, I hope she knows how much I love her, how sorry I am for all the years spent at odds with her. I hope she comes back to visit me too.

Chapter Eighteen

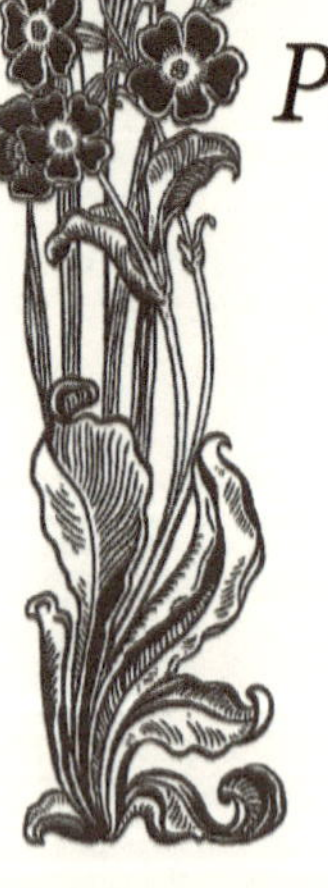

The Story of Elspet Bruce

Potions and spies

I am home and I am safe. I go out to my garden and begin to take stock of my plants, making mental notes of which ones my garden is lacking based off Aunt Agnes's instructions. Some of the plants will have to be foraged, and I need to start drying others and making tinctures and stores for my own medicine stock. I will need to do so in secret though. I fear that Aunt Agnes's worries about our future are coming true.

I am not long in the garden before my sister Mary comes to fetch me.

"Mother has a stomachache after drinking the tea you brought back and is lying down. She's asked me to have you fetch her some fresh water from the well for her," Mary says.

"I will, but I have something else to help her," I say.

I now know of something else to help her thanks to the knowledge passed down to me. I see some dandelions in the yard and begin to pick them. Aunt Agnes told me I could make a tea from them to cure certain issues with stomachs.

I pick the flowers and quickly fetch the water for Mother. As I prepare the water and tea in the kitchen, I can hear Father talking to Mary and Mother about what is happening in town.

"Elspet, come here," he says, calling me over to where they are gathered. "I want all of you to stay away from town as much as possible. Do not talk to anyone and do not gossip or inquire from others any news about the accused."

"Why Father?" Mary asks.

"More and more of our neighbors are being accused. I believe some are being accused out of revenge for slights long in the past. Others out of covetousness. I do not want to see you girls caught up in it."

Mary looks frightened, so Father takes her hands in his, then pulls her in to kiss her forehead.

"Elspet, I need you to stay here and take care of your dear mother who has taken ill," he says.

"Ill or hexed from one of those hags," Mother says.

"Do not get caught up in it," Father warns her, but she scoffs. "I do not doubt that there have been grievances and sin, but we are all sinners in the eyes of the Lord, and we are all forgiven through His son. Let us not get caught up in the hysteria and accusations."

"Father, do you not believe there are witches in Forfar?" Mary asks.

"I believe there is evil afoot, but I do not believe it is from the accused. I believe it comes from listening to the whispers of greed and fear and letting that lead them. I fear many more innocent people will be accused."

"Father," I say, "has anyone else been accused besides Mistress Helen and Isobel?"

"Mistress Helen was taken into custody and put in the tollbooth along with Mistress Isobel. Within a few hours of the witch tests beginning, they both confessed. I fear they are only the beginning, others have also been accused now and a small trickle of our neighbors have begun to fill the tollbooth."

Fear and guilt pit in my stomach. I know Tomas is the reason Mistress Helen was arrested. A fear creeps in that he may turn on me and accuse me too, but I push it away. Tomas loves me—he would never turn on me.

"It's a terrible thing, what they will do to these women," Father says. "I've seen it before, and it is not the will of God. To torture them into confession and murder them? Their sins are only for God to judge."

"Hush, Father," Mother says. "If anyone hears you saying such things then they will think you are in league with the Devil, reverend or not."

Father kisses Mother on the head, before leaving us to attend to business in town.

"Here, Mother," I say, bringing her the tea I brewed from Aunt Agnes's instructions.

"What is this?" Mother asks after taking the first sip.

"It is a tea I learned to make from Aunt Agnes. She said it would help with stomach aches."

"Elspet, you must not make any medicines or go to Aunt Agnes again," Mother warns, standing up and throwing the tea over the fire. It vaporizes with a hiss.

"Mother, stop! It is tea made from the plants the good Lord has created for us and our use. God provides, why would you just throw it out?"

"It is witchcraft, Elspet."

"You did not think so when I brought you tea from Auntie before," I say.

The pain of her hand connecting with my cheek stings badly. Before I can say anything, Mary steps in.

"Mother is right," she says. "Anyone and everyone will be watched carefully for any sign that they are in league with the Devil and a witch. Anything different, or that goes against the authority of the Minster or the Crown will be considered witchcraft. Even showing kindness to the accused will be considered a sign of guilt. We must be careful, and we must not dabble in the wicked."

"What would Father say, Mother?" I ask, still holding my cheek.

But before she can answer, I run out, chasing after Father down the dirt path that leads to town.

"Father! Father, wait!"

He stops in the middle of the path and waits as I catch up to him and reach for his arms. I am met by his embrace. Before I can say anything, he grabs my chin and inspects my cheek where Mother struck me. He leans into my ear and says, "In our time, Elspet, I see men using the word of God for evil. For the persecution and murder of those based on a judgment we are not fit to give. We will not abandon kindness, we will not abandon loving our neighbor. I know you are scared. Remember, our time upon this earth is brief, but our time after is eternal. Do not let the fear of persecution stop you from doing what is right. You must also not follow into darkness the angry and fearful mobs who accuse one another. You must not bring undue suspicion onto yourself or our family either. Lead with kindness and godliness and the Lord will protect us."

"Father, what if you knew that someone was being falsely accused because someone was trying to get rid of them? Might we speak up for the accused? Be defendants of their person?" I ask, pulling away from his embrace.

"Yes, the Lord calls upon us to bear witness to and speak the truth, but let *me* defend the good people. You and your sister must not for you will surely be accused as well. As much as I am a man of God, I am also just a man, and I cannot bear to watch my wife or daughters go through these barbaric trials. To be proven innocent is to die just as horribly as those convicted."

"But what if you knew that someone was being untruthful, that they were betraying someone you loved?" I ask timidly.

"The Lord says fear not, for I am with you; be not dismayed, for I am your God." He pulls me in for another tight hug. "Though I do not fear for myself, I do fear for you, my daughter. Your silence is your best protection."

"I promise, Father, I will be silent," I say.

It begins to rain after days of clear skies, and maybe out of habit, I go to the barn, though it no longer bears the joy and freedom on its droplets that it once did. The guilt is as heavy as the rain that pours down and I try to think of ways to help Mistress Helen. It is true, she is a wicked woman, but I do not believe her to be a witch as Tomas has accused her. I know he has only accused her so that she will not be able to tell anyone what she saw. It is one thing to pay for your own sins, but it is another to pay for the sins of others. The cramps have subsided, and my bleeding has not begun, unlike Mother whose tea appears to have worked based on the moaning coming from inside the house.

I look sadly at the pile of straw that was once the bed I shared with Tomas and begin to clean it up, moving it to the pile of old hay to be taken out of the barn and be rid of. As I rake the loose straw I jump at the touch of hands around my waist and turn, using the rake to put space between me and this interloper.

"What the hell, Elspet?" Tomas says angrily.

"I'm sorry, I didn't expect you and you scared me."

"Why didn't you expect me? It's raining."

"It's Scotland, Tomas, it rains a lot here and we don't meet every time. In fact, you've barely looked at me since last time, with Helen. It's been many days and nights."

"Don't say that witch's name lest you summon her here again," Tomas scolds.

"She's not a witch," I say.

"Yes, she is. She's already confessed to murdering her sister all those years ago. I knew she was wicked. She's also confessed to communing with the Devil with Mistress Isobel and Mistress Alexander and causing a ship to sink."

"No, that cannot be," I say. Father said they would do horrible things to the accused to force confessions. That some would confess and accept a death sentence over the continued torture. Yet she has confessed to so many things, things that cannot be proven. Is it possible she's telling the truth?

As I contemplate, Tomas approaches me, reaching out to touch my cheek.

"Worry not, my love, with the confession of her wickedness, she is sure to cause us no more problems. I am no longer a mere stable boy, not since exposing Mistress Helen. I am now part of the council of men protecting Forfar from the witches. I have power now, I have respect, and soon I will be able to leave the stables behind."

His arms once again enclose around my waist and pull me in. I turn to him and look into his deep blue eyes and smiling face. I can't help it. My heart softens and my body demands compliance to its desires. I try to resist, but my thoughts are clouded by desire and the familiarity of his body. Tomas pulls up my skirts and slides down my undergarments. He lays me down on the straw and my body acts independently, following his unspoken commands.

If the Devil is about in Forfar, I am not entirely sure that he is not in Tomas. If so, it is already too late for me. My love for Tomas has damned me. I gave in to his temptation long ago and I know I cannot stop communing with him.

God forgive me.

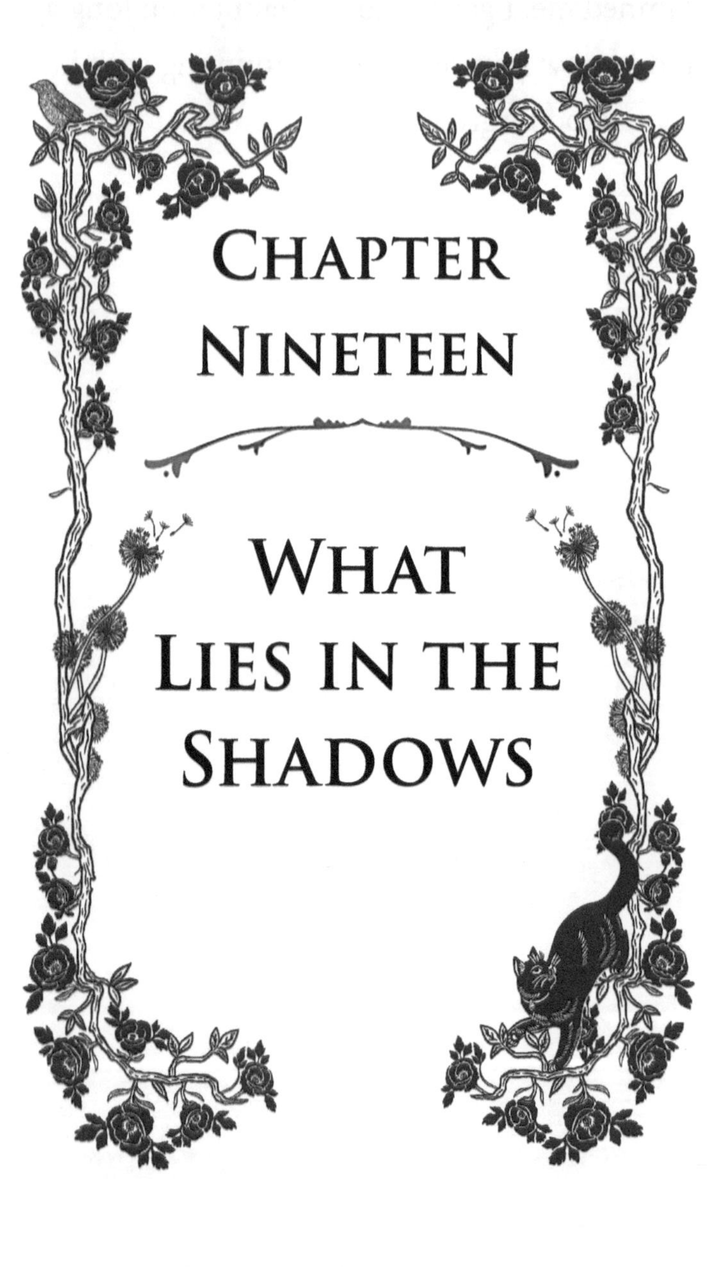

Chapter Nineteen

What Lies in the Shadows

It's been years since I last dreamed of my brother. After he died, I used to dream of him often. Sometimes he'd be sitting at the edge of my bed, smiling, waiting for me to wake up. Other times, I'd call for him frantically until I found him asleep, unable to wake up, just like all those years ago.

But this time it's different. There's no fear, no confusion, just love and peace. This time, there's a door, and my brother is walking me toward it, hand in hand. His hand feels so warm in mine. He smiles at me, urging me forward.

But as we reach the door and it begins to open, I hear someone's urgent whisper: *"Wake up."*

Panic rises in my chest. The fear floods back. I can't cross that threshold.

I let go of his hand.

When I look down at my palm, it's covered in blood.

I jolt awake, my heart racing, tears welling in my eyes. That familiar, overwhelming guilt settles over me like a heavy cloak. I sit up in bed, eyes wide in the darkness, listening for something, anything. My husband sleeps beside me, unaware.

The fear lingers. What was waiting for me on the other side of that door? I know my brother would never bring harm to me, but now there's a gnawing feeling that if I crossed with him, there would be no way back. I can't shake the thought. I can't fall back asleep. That door haunts me. What would have happened if I'd gone through?

I slip out of bed, careful not to wake my husband, my injured ankle stiff from the way I slept. I make my way to my son's room, checking on him first. His little chest rises and falls in peaceful slumber. As I watch him, a noise from my daughter's room pulls me away, and I go to check on her next.

Her blanket is bunched at the bottom of her bed, her stuffed purple hippo lying on the floor. I bend to pick it up, trying not to lose my balance. That's when I feel something brush past me—cold, a fleeting sensation that makes my skin crawl. I stand up quickly, my breath catching in my throat. I glimpse a woman in long, billowing skirts, moving past me and out the door.

Blinking, I look around. It's just me.

My heart races as I return to my daughter's bed. Her blanket is now tucked neatly around her. I freeze. Something isn't right.

I step into the hallway and see the woman's shadow moving past the doorframe to my office. Nerves spike in my stomach. I'm too scared to follow, but my feet move anyway, drawn forward.

"Elspet?" I call out.

I watch, horrified, as the shadow of her skirts moves into the closet where I'd set up an altar for Elspet. Without thinking, I rush to the closet, quickly knocking the tartan scarf out of place and slamming the door shut. The air feels heavy, thick with something dark. I step back, panic building in my chest.

Turning, I run back to my daughter's room, scoop her up, and take her into my son's room. Holding her tight, I try to calm myself. She's warm in my arms, but it doesn't help. I stay there, rocking gently in the chair, my eyes fixed on the door and hyper-alert to every sound.

I think of my mother's warnings: never open doors to the spiritual world. I should have listened. When I wanted Elspet to speak to me, it should have been to me alone, not to anyone else, least of all my children. I shouldn't have opened that book of spells. I shouldn't have tried to bind her to me. I shouldn't have invited her into my home, into my closet.

The night stretches on in a blur. I stay there, rocking, tense, on edge. When the first light of morning finally spills through the window, my body is aching and exhausted, but my mind refuses to quiet.

I hear my husband in the shower, getting ready for work. I shift carefully out of the chair, walking quietly to my daughter's room and placing her back in her bed. Stretching my back and taking a breath, I walk nervously to the office and check to make sure the closet door is still closed. Upon seeing it is still safely shut, I head to the staircase. The pain in my ankle is sharp, but I force myself to walk downstairs. One step at a time.

In the kitchen, I start the coffee and prepare breakfast for the kids. My husband joins me a few minutes later, looking just as haggard as I feel.

"Rough night?" I ask, trying to keep my voice steady.

He rubs a hand through his thick hair, yawning. "Yeah. It was weird. I don't usually dream, but last night was . . . bad. I kept tossing and turning. I couldn't get back to sleep. Usually, when you sleep in the kids' rooms, I sleep fine."

I raise an eyebrow. "I don't think I've ever known you to have a bad dream."

He shrugs. "It was a strange dream for sure. I kept hearing a woman singing a lullaby. At first, I thought it was you, but it didn't sound like you. When I sat up, the room was full of smoke, and I could see the outline of a woman, just walking in the shadows, singing. It was . . . unsettling."

My blood turns cold. I try to keep my tone neutral. "That sounds weird."

"Yeah, it was. I didn't care for it." He grabs the cup of coffee I pour for him.

"Maybe we should call a priest to bless the house." I look at him seriously. "We should."

He laughs, shaking his head. "We can if it makes you feel better. Bad dreams happen, though."

He's right, I suppose. Bad dreams do happen, more often for some than others. I want to tell him that I don't think this is random, that it's connected to something deeper, but he wouldn't believe me. He'd think I'm overreacting, or worse, he'd worry and push me to talk to someone again.

The rest of the morning passes in its usual blur—making lunches, fighting with hairbrushes, giving hugs and kisses goodbye—but now there's an added weight, the sore stiffness of my ankle, the dread still lingering.

I consider taking the day off from work to

try and rest, but I need to save my vacation time for the holidays. So, I log in, sorting through the overflowing inbox, trying to focus. But all I can think about is Elspet. The closet door keeps drawing my gaze.

It's too much. I need to do something. I need to break this.

I spend my lunch hour researching how to cleanse the house, trying to find something that will lift this feeling. I come across the practice of saining, a Scottish ritual similar to smudging, except using juniper branches instead of sage. But I have no idea where to find juniper, and filling the house with smoke would not go over well with my husband.

Then I find an article on using lemons for purification. I have lemons. I slice them, sprinkle salt inside the wedges, and place them above my front door. I'm tempted to throw them in the closet too, but something holds me back.

I don't feel ready to close that door, not yet. I need Elspet's help.

Satisfied with the lemons, I sit down with a cup of warm tea in my hands. For the first time in hours, the air feels lighter. Maybe today won't be so bad after all.

Chapter Twenty

Charms for Luck and Charms for Protection

The day went by quickly and I felt extremely productive having cleared my inbox and list of actions at work. I was foolish to think it would last or that the lemons would be enough. The call came in while I was taking a shower after logging off for the day. An accident on the playground had left my daughter with a possible sprained arm. I decided to rush and pick her up rather than have them take a scary ride without me in the ambulance.

Four hours later, after some X-rays in the ER, we learn Audrey has a hairline fracture in her collarbone and will be in a sling for the next six to twelve weeks. It feels like my fault, even though I know I couldn't have prevented it since I wasn't there. When I finally meet my husband and son at home, both my daughter and I are emotionally and physically drained.

My husband frustrates me with his unserious attitude about the broken bone.

"Maybe we should homeschool her," I suggest.

"Sure, just pay off all your credit cards, quit shopping and eating out, and in a few years, you can stay home," he responds.

"Why are you such an asshole?" I snap.

"Why do you always go to extremes?" he retorts. "It was an accident. She's a kid, accidents happen. I remember being a kid, and every year at least one kid had a cast on. Kids are supposed to play and occasionally get hurt. It's a rite of passage. Don't you remember comparing battle scars as a kid?"

It's true. I also broke my collarbone as a child, trying to flip a swing but managing to only collapse the whole set on top of myself.

"She isn't supposed to get a broken bone at school," I counter. "They are supposed to be keeping her safe."

"Okay, so should we order a bubble to put her in?"

"I hate you," I mutter, walking away and putting the kettle on to boil for another cup of tea.

"No, you don't," he says, wrapping his arms around my waist from behind and planting a kiss on my neck.

I wonder if this is how Elspet felt when Tomas tried to discredit her fears and her concerns about what was to come.

We're interrupted by the whistle of the kettle. I pull it off the stove, breaking free from his embrace, and head to the drawer where I keep my tea bags. As I search for the black tea, I spot the box of mugwort I bought. My hand lingers on it for a moment before I grab the black tea and shut the drawer.

"That's your problem," he says, pointing at the tea.

"Excuse me?" I reply, feeling annoyed.

"It's eight p.m. Why are you drinking caffeine? This is why you have trouble sleeping and so much anxiety. All you drink is tea all day."

"It relaxes me."

"The caffeine doesn't relax you. Your last cup should be at noon, not eight."

We argue for a bit about whether it's my habits or the school's negligence to blame. My husband sides with the daycare, and the conversation ends with him heading to bed while I slice more lemons to place along the door and window frames.

When I'm finished, I fire up my laptop at the kitchen table to talk to Elspet. I feel like she's truly the only one who understands.

CHAPTER TWENTY-ONE

THE STORY OF ELSPET BRUCE

The Devil in the details

I t wasn't long after Mistress Helen was accused and arrested that the first execution took place. It was Isobel. I heard from Father that they had tortured her in unspeakable manners until she finally confessed to the charges levied against her. He said anyone would confess under such duress to stop the interrogation. Needles slowly inserted into different parts of her skin, looking for a spot that didn't hurt to prove she was in league with the Devil. Father told us to stay away from town on the day of her execution, and truly I meant to. I had planned to check on Aunt Agnes.

But walking on the path toward her house, I feel the shock of a hand around my waist and one against my mouth. I try to scream but my lips are locked by the force of the hand clamped over them.

My body hurts as I rail against the hands that hold me, that drag me off the path and into the woods. I kick in desperation despite the protest of my tired legs.

I fight, but the tethers of his arms are too strong.

Then laughter rings out. The familiarity does nothing to calm me down. It's not until the hands release me and I turn to face my attacker that I realize it is Tomas.

"Tomas, what are you playing at?" I yell.

He laughs again and pulls me into him.

"Don't be cross lass, I am only playing with you a little." He smells lightly of drink.

"What are you doing out here?" I question, pushing him away.

He laughs again and pulls his shirt off, then comes to give me another kiss. I don't want him, I don't want to have this desire, but I do and give into his kiss. He grabs the back of my head aggressively and pulls me hard against him. He works to undress me and pulls me down onto the cool ground of the forest. It isn't long into our romp before I start to feel a tingling sensation in my bottom and my back. I try to ignore it, but the feeling keeps nagging me. Soon the tingling turns into a burning.

"Tomas, get off."

He is lost in his passion and ignores me.

"Tomas, please, I am burning!" I yell.

"Me too," he says with a moan.

I try to shove him off, but he is too heavy. I am left to wait for it to finally be over. When Tomas rolls off me, I sit up and turn to see in horror that he laid us in a bed of stinging nettles. Tomas, dulled by his drink, must not have seen or felt it yet. He feels it now as he begins to grab at his face and arms.

"What have you done to me, witch?" he asks.

"What have I done?" I say angrily. "You are the one who made us a bed of nettles. Come, let us go to Mistress Agnes, she will be able to stop the stinging and itching."

I put my clothes back on and reach for his hand, but he smacks me away and walks off, mumbling and shooting me an angry look. Hurt, angry, and a bit shamed, I make my way to Aunt

Agnes's house alone.

As I get closer, I catch the scent of burning wood. Soon I see heavy smoke rising above the tree line. This should not be. Fear pits in my stomach and I break into a run.

"Auntie?" I yell. "Auntie?"

There is no response.

When I get there, her house is empty and her hut is nothing but a ruin of smoke and ash. Her garden has been destroyed. I know what happened and who is responsible. I know now why Tomas was out this way and why he smelled of drink. I know in the deepest part of that this was his doing. I should have heeded Father's warning, but I needed to see her, I needed to know she was okay.

I walk as quickly as I can without full-on running to the tollbooth in town where Father said they were keeping the accused. I am overwhelmed with a sense of impending dread the closer I get. I can hear the commotion of the crowd that has gathered. The cries to kill the witches, to send them back to Hell. My throat feels tight as I try to peer around the spectators, looking for Aunt Agnes. What I see instead is Mistress Isobel tied to a chair. The counselor is there, along with the reverend whom my father falls under, a man of the Old Testament, without love and full of vengeance against all women and any type of sin. They have already tied a rope around her neck and begun to pull it tightly. Her eyes bulge and her face turns bright red as the crowd cheers. It feels like forever for Mistress Isobel to stop squirming in her iron seat, to stop fighting the rope.

When her movements finally slow, the men bring forth a large hot cauldron of black liquid. From the smell and the way it pours out thickly from the pot onto Mistress Isobel, I could see it is tar. The heat against her skin is enough to revive her slightly from the entanglement of the rope. She makes gurgles and weak movements against the black mass of liquid that engulfs her until she finally sits motionless. I thank God it was over for her. I pray that her soul will quickly be taken far from this place, which seems much more like Hell to me than what Father described from his good book.

With the show over, the crowd begins to disperse.

I look desperately for Aunt Agnes, growing bolder and walking toward the bars that hold the accused women inside.

"Aunt Agnes?" I call out softly, hoping for her to hear but not others.

"What are you doing here?" one of the guards asks, catching me. I stay silent out of fear. "Have ye come to commune with your fellow witches?"

"No, I, I . . ."

"Elspet, there you are," I hear a familiar voice call out. "You should know better than to let your curiosity get the better of you. No doubt that is what led some of these women straight to the Devil himself and damned them to Hell. Let's be off, I'll take you to your mother who will be none too happy to hear you've been poking around where you shouldn't."

The voice belongs to Alfred, a friend of my parents. As he grabs my arm to pull me away, another harsh and bony hand grabs my wrist from behind the bars.

"Tell them what you saw girl, or I shall tell them what I did see," the gravelly voice of Mistress Helen rings out.

Before I can say anything, another hand shoots out, tearing Mistress Helen's touch away from me. I see it is Aunt Agnes, with a dirty and swollen face.

"Leave the child be, Helen. She dwells in the light where we can only dwell in shadows. Any image you may have seen of her was me casting it."

"So you say Mistress Agnes, but there is a mark on the lass, one not conjured by you," Helen says.

It feels as if the Devil himself is casting his shadow over me. I freeze. She has seen the birthmark on my inner thigh that no one but my mother should know about. The one that Tomas knows well.

"What are you saying, witch?" the guard interrupts, coming toward the bars of the tollbooth and knocking his sword loudly against the bars.

"Let's go now," Alfred says quietly, pulling me away as the guard eyes me with suspicion.

As I let him lead me from that place, his arm protectively around me, I see Tomas at the crossroads, his eyes still glassy from drink, his face and arms red from the nettles. I give him a pleading look but am met with hard eyes that refuse to meet mine. As we pass him, I see him mouth the word *witch*.

I allow Alfred to guide me home and watch as Tomas approaches the guards. A feeling of dread once again overwhelms me, and I fear what is to come. I fear I will soon face a reckoning for my own sins, for my own silence. I know in my soul that things are going to get worse.

Who can I tell, who can I warn without damning myself? They will think me a witch and I too will burn if I tell them the truth. I cannot save Aunt Agnes, I can only damn myself—and with me, my family.

Alfred is met at the door by my mother. Her face goes from surprise to worry when she sees us together.

"I found this one getting too close to the fire burning in town," he says.

"I'll go get my husband," my mother says, grabbing my arm and pulling me inside. Then she reaches out to gently touch his arm. "Alfred, do come in. It's time we make the announcement."

"What announcement, Mother?" I ask.

Mother, ignoring my question, wastes no time admonishing me as she calls for Father. I sit quietly waiting for him to come talk to me after he is done with Alfred.

Father doesn't look at me at first. He keeps his back to me, looking at our bookcase, the holy book in his hand.

"Father," I start to say but he silences me. "Father, forgive me—"

"You are to be a wife now, Elspet. To Master Alfred. As such, you will stay away from town, from the gardens and herbs."

"What?" It feels as though I've fallen into icy waters. How could this be?

He quickly turns to me and holds his finger to my lips.

"Elspet, I know. I always have. The Devil has ears to hear and eyes to see, just as God does. It's to God you make your penance, but you do so in a manner that does not play into the Devil's hand, do you understand?" he asks, his eyes pleading, and I nod. "You will marry Master Alfred as your mother has arranged. You will be a good and dutiful wife. You will forget everything your aunt has taught you."

"But Father?" I say, fighting back the tears that begin to well in my eyes.

"No," he says.

"Father, Aunt Agnes is innocent."

"Of being a witch, yes, I believe she is. But she has already confessed. I do believe it was in an attempt to spare others, but it is in vain. She will die, horribly so. As will the others. So will you if you do not keep your head about you, if you do not heed my warnings. If you do not marry Master Alfred."

I fight my body's desire to crumple upon the floor. It feels as though thoughts are being trapped in mud as I struggle to think clearly. As my world collapses, I fight to be strong like my aunt. The woman who should have been my mother.

"Father, can I bring her some holy water, for protection?"

"For protection, or as a charm?" Father asks.

I know what he means. They will see it as an act of witchcraft and guilt. I can't help but feel an impending sense of doom. Aunt Agnes is in the tollbooth accused, Mistress Helen seems ready to accuse me as well. If Tomas was not already angry at me, he will be once he hears I am to marry Master Alfred. I feel like my days are numbered. Tomas will surely come for vengeance.

Chapter Twenty-Two

Blessings and Spells

Holy water. I thank Elspet for giving me an answer. I hurry up the stairs as quickly as my leg will allow and into my son's room. In his closet, I struggle to quietly pull down his giant blue memory box without waking him. I lay it on the floor and rummage through it until I find what I'm searching for—the bottle of holy water from his baptism.

Grabbing it, I get up and walk to my son's window. I sprinkle some water on the windowsill, then move to the door, dribbling some on the threshold. I continue throughout the house, room by room, sprinkling the blessed water on every windowsill and door frame. It's nearly midnight by the time I make it to the basement to finish. I beg God to protect our family from evil.

As I look around, the bottle now three-quarters empty, it comes to me: I should sprinkle some on myself and my family. And so I do, first on my children, who stir slightly from the cold sensation. But my husband wakes up when I accidentally drop the bottle, spilling its contents on his face.

"Dammit," I mutter.

"Nina, what the hell!" he yells, sitting up. He grabs the bottle. "Did you just pour holy water on me? What the actual fuck is going on?" His voice is full of anger as he jumps out of bed, pulls off his shirt, and tosses it into the laundry bin by the closet. He grabs a new shirt.

"You are making a big deal out of a small spill of water," I say, but am met with a dirty look. "With everything that's been going on—your nightmare, our daughter's injury—I was just trying to keep our family safe."

"I can't," he says, and I feel both anger and tears rise within me. "You have to talk to someone. I don't doubt that you're fighting some demons, but they're your demons, and you need help. If not for your sake, then for the sake of our family. Our marriage, our children. We can't continue like this. I'll even go with you."

"Why don't you believe me?" I yell, frustration overtaking me. "You've never believed me." My voice breaks. "You've always thought I was crazy. But I'm not crazy! I see things, I hear things, I dream things. I have feelings, and they are real! Just like my mother, just like my grandmother, just like Elspet."

"Like Elspet?" he repeats, confused.

"Nina, this has gone too far," he says. "This was supposed to be a healthy distraction, an outlet, not an obsession. Please," he begs, "promise me you'll call someone, or I will."

I love him, but I can see it in his eyes. I'll never make him see, never make him believe.

"I promise I'll call tomorrow to make an appointment," I reassure.

With his anger fading into frustration and concern, he leaves me and goes to sleep in our guest room for the remainder of the night.

Grabbing my laptop, I open up Elspet and silently ask her to help me.

Chapter Twenty-Three

The Story of Elspet Bruce

Everything

wilts

A Witch's Penance

istress Isobel's dying face haunts my dreams and Mistress Helen haunts my thoughts. I feel as though her presence is lurking in every shadow, though I know she is locked up in the tollbooth. Father has forbidden me from going back into town after Alfred dragged me home and our betrothal was announced. He has ordered me to stay within the bounds of our property. I wish I could see Aunt Agnes, to bring her some comfort if not some hope, but Father says it is too late. She confessed and has been sentenced to death. He believes it was a bid to save others. I know it was to save me. The guilt weighs heavily, filling my stomach with knots and I am unable to eat. Mistress Helen has accused more women from town of being in her coven and I know my days are numbered.

It is raining again, but it brings me dread instead of excitement. Tomas has not come to me in our barn since Master Alfred brought me home to Father. I know there is nothing for me in the barn, I know I should never want to see

Tomas again, but I can't help myself from sneaking away. Gathering my skirts, I leap across the growing puddles, failing and stepping in the muddy waters. My feet are immediately cold and wet.

The barn smells musty and damp from the ceaseless rain this past week. I close the door and am caught off guard by a painfully tight grip on my arm that swings me around. I am hit with the pungent scent of stale whisky and see the face of my assailant is my once dear Tomas.

"Tomas?" I say, wriggling my arm free of his grip. I am met by a shove from his hands, which sends me tumbling back into a pile of hay. "Tomas, stop, you're hurting me." I scramble to my feet and stand as tall as I can, but I'm no match for his height.

"You have hurt me, witch!" he says, pacing back and forth angrily like a mad dog. "How long have you been running around with Master Alfred on me?"

"I don't know what you mean," I say.

"I saw you two in town, the way you ran off together arm in arm."

"Tomas, he was bringing me home back to my father after Mistress Helen suggested I was a witch. He was protecting me while you stood back, silent."

"Are you telling me that you are not betrothed then?" he asks angrily.

"Tomas, it is not my will."

"You are a witch," he says. "You bewitched me and now have set your claws into Master Alfred. You are a succubus just as Mistress Helen says."

"What are you talking about? None of this would be happening if you hadn't lied and accused her of witchcraft because she caught us in the barn. This is your fault, you are the one who has lied and sinned and now the blood of innocent women is on your hands! None of this would have happened if you had made me a proper wife from the start instead of making me wait for a fortune that is never to come!" I say, almost yelling at him and revealing our forbidden meeting.

"No. You put me under a spell. You commanded me to accuse her."

"No, I didn't. You're drunk, Tomas."

Tomas grabs my shoulders and pushes me against the barn wall. His dirty hand caresses the side of my face. "You are too beautiful to be a witch. You would not betray me, would you?"

"Of course not," I stammer.

"This is Master Alfred's fault. He made you turn against me. Do not worry, my love, I will make sure he never comes between us again."

He presses against me, but I fight to resist his forced kiss, pushing him off.

"Tomas, enough," I protest.

He wanders out of the barn, saying, "Do not worry, my love, I will free you of his evil."

Breathless and in fear, I thank the Lord when he left. He has become a monster, far from the man I fell in love with, and I wonder how much of this change is my fault. Something changed in him the day Mistress Helen saw us. Maybe she is a witch, maybe she is responsible for all the misfortune befalling our town. It would be so easy to blame her, but I think of my father, of his teachings, and I cannot remove my own sin and fault from this. Maybe it is time for a confession. To come forth with the truth of my sins with Tomas and the innocence of Mistress Helen.

I leave the barn and go back to the house, looking for Father.

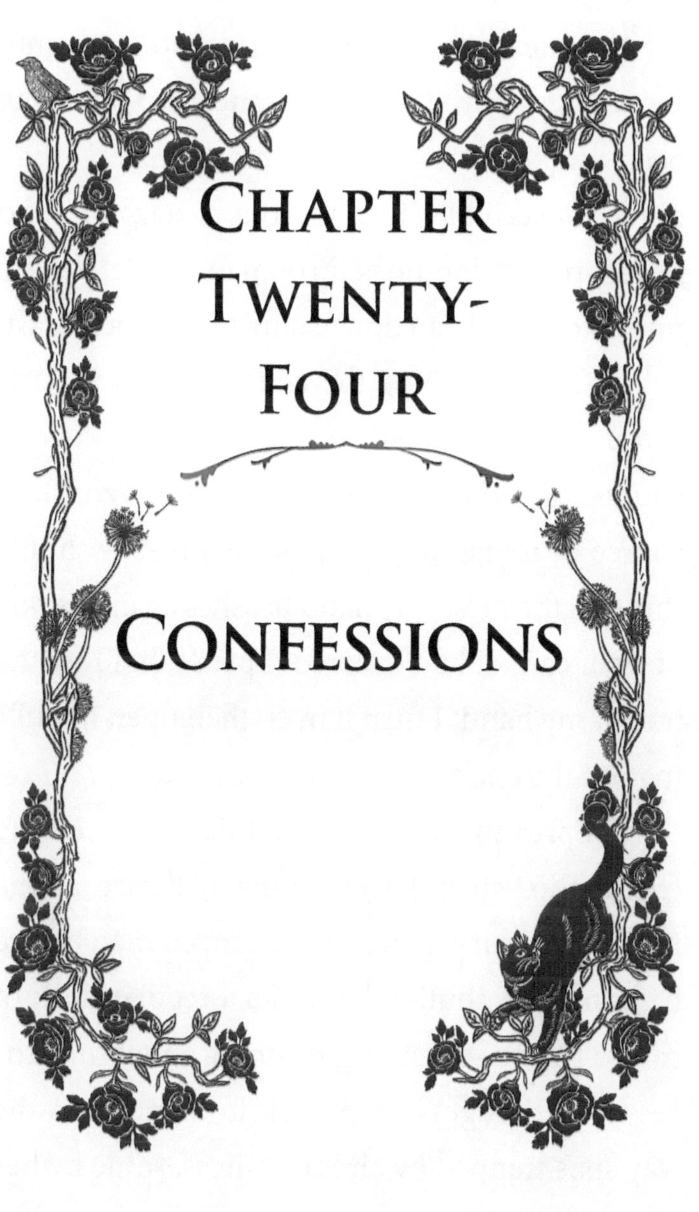

Chapter Twenty-Four

Confessions

The chirping of my husband's alarm pulls me from Elspet's world and back into my own. It's six a.m., and despite having been awake all night, I feel more anxious than tired. He stumbles into the room, haggard, and heads straight for the bathroom to shower. I close my laptop and head downstairs to start breakfast.

After brewing the coffee and setting the kettle to boil, I begin organizing the kitchen counter, which is always cluttered, a constant source of irritation to my husband. As I shuffle through the mess, my hand brushes against a box of tarot cards I had ordered. I pause, holding the box in my hand. I turn it over, then open it, pulling out the deck.

Spreading the cards out like I've seen my friends do when I was younger, I gaze at the images of a fairy queen and a hanged man before beginning to shuffle them like a regular deck of cards. There's something soothing about the process. My thoughts drift back to Elspet and the way she's trapped by circumstances, some by her own doing, others completely beyond her control. I understand the desperate desire to escape, to correct everything that went wrong.

Warm hands slide over my stomach, pulling me gently into my husband's embrace. He presses a light kiss to my temple, reaffirming the trust I have in him, that he will always stand by me, no matter what. I can't help but wonder how different things might have been for Elspet, for my family, if she had the same kind of support I do in my partner.

"I love you," he whispers in my ear.

I squeeze his hand, which rests on my stomach. I'm still holding onto the tarot deck with my other hand.

"I love you too," I reply softly.

There's a calmness in the air this morning. The usual chaos of our routine feels muted, despite the disruption of my late-night holy water dowsing. Maybe it actually worked, and the calmness is a result of the evil and negativity being temporarily held at bay. I know it's not a permanent solution. The water is all used up now.

With my children and husband off to school and work, I make myself a cup of mugwort tea, dreamer's tea, and bring the tarot deck to my office. I grab my phone from the charger and send a text to my supervisor, letting them know I'm taking another sick day. I can tell their patience is wearing thin with my frequent time off.

I set my tea and phone on the desk, then start shuffling the tarot cards again, focusing on Elspet. As I shuffle, a card slips from the deck, floating to the floor. I pick it up and see that it's the Judgment card.

Chapter Twenty-Five

The Story of Elspet Bruce

God is my witness

I hadn't expected to see Mother when I ran into the house for Father. She is usually out running errands in town on this day. I certainly hadn't expected to see Master Alfred, much less all of him as he and Mother engaged in acts reserved for marriage.

No sooner had I seen them did I cover my mouth to hold in the shock that wished to escape me. I quickly tried to back out of the room, but Mother's eyes locked with mine and I froze.

She smiled at me, like a cat who had gotten away with all the milk in the pale. Carrying on with Alfred as if I were not there. Once I had my wits about me, I managed to quietly back out of the room, shut the door, and run.

At first, I did not know where I was running, but soon the familiar path and scent of old firewood surrounded me, and I arrived at Aunt Agnes's ruined home.

I kneeled before the scorched earth, soaked and cold from the rain that continued to fall. Everything around me was dark and painted in shades of decay and death. I placed my hands on the ground before me and felt something hard and cold in the earth. It was Aunties Necklace, the iron cross my uncle had made for her. The chain was broken, likely lost when they came to arrest her.

Holding the cross in my hand, I didn't know what else to do, so I prayed.

"Father, please . . . God as my witness, I meant no harm to anyone or anything. If I could take everything back now, I would. Innocent people are dying because of me. Because of my actions, because of my desires. My selfishness."

"I knew you were in league with the Devil, witch."

I turn to see Tomas, and with him is my mother. As they step further into the clearing of what was Aunt Agnes's house, I see that there are others behind them. Tomas comes toward me, and I struggle to stand up.

"Tomas, no," I say as he grabs my hair and pushes me back down to kneeling.

"Here she is, at the site of another witch and praying to the Devil."

"Mother!" I cry out.

She walks over to me. "I knew from the moment you were born you were hers. The only time you didn't cry as a babe was when you were in her arms. I should have left you to her then," she says.

"I know your secrets too, Mother," I say through gritted teeth.

"Yes, but you wouldn't," she replies.

The town guard approaches through the crowd and my wrists are tied together.

"Mistress Helen has provided proof of your witchcraft, along with Tomas," the guard says. "You will be given a trial. Until then, you will remain in the tollbooth with the other accused witches."

The mud is thick from the rain and my feet slip and sink in as I stumble along the torn-up path from my aunt's to the tollbooth. Mother's words echo in my head the whole way. *But you wouldn't.*

Chapter
Twenty-Six

Atonement

Elspet believed her actions had unleashed the Devil, and maybe they had. Once Pandoras box was opened by her and Tomas, there was no way to pull all the evil that was unleashed back in and seal it again. Not in her time, at least. But I can.

As my determination grows and courage courses through me, my phone rings. It's my mother. I silence it, but it immediately rings again.

"Hello?" I answer, annoyance creeping into my voice.

"Nina, listen. I'm on my way to the hospital. Your grandmother had another stroke. I had to call an ambulance," she says.

"Is she going to be okay?" I ask, concern rushing in. I begin to search for my keys and purse.

"I'm not sure, but you know her, she always manages to come back from Death's door. You don't need to come down. I'll call you once I know what's going on. I love you, okay?" she says before hanging up.

"I already halfway out the door, Mom," I say. "I'm coming."

"Nina, stop," She says sternly. "There is nothing you can do here but get in the way right now. Stay home, hug the babies and wait, okay?"

With my feelings stung, I wonder if this is the curse, trying to distract me now that I am finally getting close. I will not be distracted.

I finish my tea and, ignoring my mother's warning about using such things, I grab the deck of cards. Leaving the office for my bedroom, I begin to shuffle, saying, "Show me how to break the curse." I lie down on my bed, continuing to shuffle the cards. After a moment, I hear what sounds like my name being called, but it's barely a whisper. I push it aside, refocusing on my intention: to break the curse, to free Elspet, to free my family. To free myself.

I don't need the book to interpret the cards for me, I can feel what they are telling me to do. In order to break the curse, in order to make things right, I need to confront the curse itself, I need to go to Forfar and end the cycle of misfortune. I need to kill the curse.

I run downstairs and grab my wallet, then quickly look up flights to Scotland. I text my husband that I have taken our talk last night seriously and am booking myself for a weekend retreat. Before he can respond, I turn off my phone and shove it in my back pocket, lock up the house and head to the airport, grabbing only my purse and passport. Elspet's mother's words echo in my head now: *but you wouldn't*. I will do what Elspet couldn't. I will show her mother that I would, and I will. Clutching the cross necklace, I swear upon it that I will help my grandmother come back from death's door.

CHAPTER TWENTY-SEVEN

THE STORY OF ELSPET BRUCE

Truths

unspoken

I've lost count of how many weeks I have been in the tollbooth. It is far worse than I feared it would be. The coldness is that of which I have never felt before, it settles in my bones and threatens to make them as fragile as newly formed ice. The dampness has seeped into everything, it makes the air thick and worsens the stench of human waste, sweat and fear. It is also crowded with other women and children, some of whom I recognize, and some I do not. There is nothing but misery here, but I resolve to tell the truth when it is my turn for interrogation. I await my turn in the sunless dungeon for days, watching the other women be taken out in hysterics and brought back broken, bruised, and bloodied. But worse than this is the women who do not return, for I know they have been found guilty. Strangled and burned in tar like Mistress Isobel. After spending so much time in the dark hell hole of the tollbooth, sometimes death seems like a relief, like a mercy.

I don't sleep much but when I do, I am

haunted by the faces of the women around me, of Tomas, and of Mistress Helen who sleeps on the other side of the tollbooth. I hide from Mistress Helen, doing my best to keep her from noticing me. These nightmares feel more real each night and I wake up in panic with the taste of dirt in my mouth, and the lingering feel of a hand clasped tightly over it, muffling any screams. I hear the voice of my mother whisper in my ear. She tells me I will not die, that I will live to see my freedom from the tollbooth. But not my freedom from her or the curse she lays upon me. She will not give me the chance to cleanse my sin, to utter my truths or my apologies. I struggle to call out, to ask her why. Then I see it. It plays in my head like a memory. Mother was young, and she would meet with her own Tomas in the barn on rainy days. I was always told that I came early—now it makes sense. Mother married Father out of necessity, because she was pregnant with me. I am the blame she names.

"Wake up," Mistress Helen says.

I open my eyes to find her face inches from mine.

"You've been haunted since the day you were born. They can say what they want about me, but at least I love my child."

"What are you talking about?" I ask, confused.

"You're a child without a mother's love. Think hard about it, lass. You've always known this," she replies.

I stare at her, and suddenly, I realize the truth in her words, I see it on her face, in her eyes. I feel it from her soul as I reach out and touch her arm.

"What will you do?" she asks, her voice soft but insistent.

"Nothing," I say, pulling my hand back and resting against the wall of the tollbooth, my own voice hollow. Every choice I've made has led me to this moment, the toll of someone's life lost, and now, perhaps, my own. "My mother is wicked, but I won't betray her or my father and sister. Too many women have died here already. I cannot bear to be the reason more are added to the pyre."

"You love her despite everything," she observes.

"I love my family. It's not a choice," I say, the weight of it heavy in my chest. I run my fingers repeatedly over my aunt's cross that I have kept hidden in the folds of my skirt. My heart breaking that she is no longer here to wear it.

"There are many things that lead a person to wickedness, some of it for our own vices, some of it for others," she continues, pulling back her ragged shawl to reveal a sleeping child on her lap, her daughter. I spent so much time avoiding Mistress Helen, I had missed the child she was trying to shield from the horrors within our prison. "Sometimes, we don't realize until it's too late that our anger, our fear, is really just grief. I thought I could save her, my sweet child," she adds softly.

I look at this woman, evil incarnate, the

one responsible for so many deaths, and for the first time, I understand why. My body trembles, and tears spill from my eyes. This grief will haunt me for the rest of my life, however short it may be. And the daughters in my bloodline, starting with the one I carry in my womb from Tomas, will know this pain too. We will all know heartache. We will all know heartbreak. We will live in fear of the shadow that will follow us.

"Will you forgive me?" I ask her.

She sits quietly for a moment, then looks are her daughter and firmly says, "No."

I fight to break free of this suffocating grip. I struggle to push the dirt from my mouth but realize there is none. Mistress Helen just laughs.

"There's no use in fighting it, lass. You must simply let it be," she says, her voice filled with dark amusement.

I clutch my womb, nausea rising within me. I fear for the poor, wretched soul trapped inside.

Chapter Twenty-Eight

Acts of Forgiveness

I couldn't sleep on the plane. My body has been pushed beyond exhaustion as I park at the entrance to the park in Forfar. I turn my phone on to use the navigation, finally reaching my destination, ignoring the dozens of notifications from my husband and mother, both of whom have been trying to reach me.

My throat feels tight, and my head burns as I make my way toward the Forfar memorial stone that lay under a large Hawthrone tree. Each step feels heavy, as though I'm walking through a fierce wind, though none blows. The tree beneath which the stone sits is in bloom. I can tell even in the darkness. The large stone reads, "Forfar witches / Just people," but I know that's not entirely true. They were more than just people. They were daughters, mothers, and they were all victims, each one, even the ones who passed on the cruelty to others.

I can feel her, Helen. Or her ghost. I can feel all the ghosts of those accused and murdered. They are no longer hiding in the shadows, but hovering over me, trying to hold me back with an unmovable weight of unresolved grief, of anger. It threatens to block me from my path, but still, I trudge on.

As I get closer to the stone, the weight of what I'm doing presses down, threatening to crush me. My skin burns, and the pain in my head screams. When I finally reach the stone, I collapse before it. My head feels as though it will burst, and I'm certain I will lose consciousness. But I know I must carry out this task. I know what is at stake if I don't.

Still kneeling, I place one hand on the stone and the other over my heart.

"By the power of the precious blood, by the holy name of Jesus, I cast out the curse laid upon me and my family." I feel as though a massive stone is gradually pressing more and more weight onto my chest.

"I am sorry for the part my ancestor played." I continue to fight to get the words out as the cross necklace feels as though it is tightening.

"Most of all, I forgive Elspet."

The burning sensation fades from my body, the searing pain in my head dissipates. I sink to the ground, breathless. From the shadows, by each rock of the ring that circles the memorial, the outlines of those who were murdered begin to appear. I see Helen, her figure the darkest of them all, circling the perimeter like a cat.

Then I see Elspet. She moves toward me with a gentle smile. Tears spill from my eyes as my heart begins to beat harder, faster. A new pain fills my chest. Elspet is surrounded by light, and she holds out her hand for me to take. Behind her, a door begins to open. I reach for her hand, and as I step toward the door, I'm met by the warm, familiar presence of my brother, who also offers me his hand. Together, the three of us step toward the door.

But then a voice calls to me urgently.

"Nina," it says. "Wake up."

I sit up, disoriented, the shadows surrounding me once again. I hear the laughter of a woman in the dark, and I know it's Helen. It feels like an eternity before the shadows start to clear, and my room takes focus.

It was a dream. All of it was a dream.

But I know Elspet is still there, lurking in the shadows. I can feel her, her eyes still watching me. I can feel the weight of her sorrow.

I never left the lion's den. No angel walks beside me. But I am not alone, even though I am still damned. I can feel Elspet with me. I feel her in me, her blood, her memory, running through my veins, embedded in my DNA. I am no longer afraid of my gifts. I embrace them. And in doing so, I can see her clearly now. I am no longer afraid to walk through that door the next time it's offered to me. I know what Elspet is telling me to do, what I must do. *Forgive myself.*

Chapter Twenty-Nine

All the World is a Lie

The world is full of lies. Some are those told to us by others, like how we're told our heart resides under our left breast when the truth is that it lies in the center. We believe it, because there is rarely a reason for us to check the lie, to believe it to be false. The lies we tell ourselves, those are the strongest, and often the most damning. The truth often lies in the center of all things. The Devil serves to distract, to lead us away from our center. To create fantasies and altered visions of the truth.

I have been distracted for far too long by the fear of what could be, instead of the truth of what is. God says not to fear the unknown or the future, but to trust in Him. It is time that I started to trust, and time that I started embracing the truth and my gift.

The truth I now realize is that Helen was a victim as much as Elspet. That Elspet's mother was an angry bitch who is to blame, if anyone, for the start of the family curse. That the trauma, the guilt, that passed from Elspet to her daughter, and so forth down the family line is not because of the iron cross. It is because of the unresolved grief and shame passed down through our blood memories. But no longer. It ends with me.

I know what I must do, and I am no longer afraid. I will break this curse through forgiveness and through truth. Some confessions cannot just be said—they must be lived.

I don't need to travel to Forfar to set things right. I don't need to face down the demons of our family's past either. I only need to face myself, my own truth, and my own gifts. Forgiveness will start with me, and it is forgiveness that I will pass on to my daughter along with the cross necklace. I know now it is a symbol of love, of strength, and of sacrifice.

Chapter Thirty

The Confession of Elspet Bruce

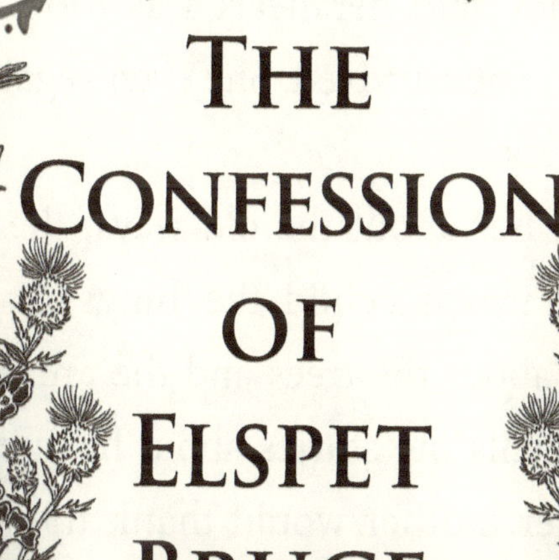

I visit Grandmother often in hospice, where the doctors say the stroke is too much for her to overcome. I don't believe them, though. We've been told many times before that she was going to die. Like the time she fell and broke her hip, and they said her heart was too weak for surgery. But she survived. She even regained her ability to walk.

I ask her about the old ways, the life she had on the farm as a child, the things her mother taught her about the trees and the animals. She smiles and tells me stories about her pet skunk and how her mother would thank the trees for their protection.

"What kind of trees did she talk to?" I ask.

"Oh, all kinds," Grandmother replies. "A weeping willow was her favorite. And a strong, tall oak with a funny face in the bark that only her and I could see."

"A face?" I ask, intrigued.

"Yes, don't you remember?" she says, her voice growing tired. "Your peonies were always my favorite." She's confusing me for her mother again. "You had every shade and color, and when they bloomed, it was like a rainbow lining the long drive."

"That sounds beautiful," I say, not correcting her.

Her eyes flutter shut. "It was, Mom." Her voice is soft now, the words slurring.

I spend the rest of my visits cherishing what wisdom she has left to offer. I let the rain, the earth, and the plants remain my friends and my source of healing, just as I believe they were for Grandmother and Elspet. They call to me, and I will answer. I walk into my yard, up to the old silver maples that stand like sentinels, asking them to protect my land and my family. I ask them to weave their roots into a barrier, to keep out negativity and evil.

But there are two trees missing from my yard, two that I know I need. A hawthorn tree, like the one at the Forfar memorial, a tree symbolizing the healing of one's heart. And a rowan tree, known for its protective properties. Neither is something I can pick up at the nursery, but I can order them, and so I do.

It takes three weeks for the trees to arrive. In that time, Grandmother has become increasingly tired and sleeps most of the day. The crows she used to watch from my window still come by, and I offer them small gifts of seeds and dimes when they do.

Though the nursery offers to plant the trees for me, I know it's something I must do myself. I begin the work, digging into the earth with care and thoughtfulness, with clear intentions. Even once they are planted, I know my work isn't done.

Elspet's sins are not mine, but I carry her blood and the memories it has passed down through the generations. It is not my cross to bear, but I cannot deny the imprint her actions left on me and my family. I kneel before the young hawthorn tree and lay my hand gently upon its trunk. There is one last chapter in the story of Elspet, but it is one I will not write. Instead, I look up to the sky, and as the rain begins to fall, I offer this confession in place of my ancestor.

"I do solemnly confess, in the shadow of my own sins and the light of divine judgment, that I willingly succumbed to wickedness with Tomas. That when Mistress Helen did chance upon us and beheld our union. Tomas, in his dark heartedness, did threaten her with dire consequences should she reveal what she had seen, and she, in her fear, did vow silence.

"We continued our meetings in the secrecy of my father's barn and once amidst the woods, indulging in our grievous sin of lies and deceit at the expense of others. Tomas, in a vile attempt to conceal our transgressions, did accuse Mistress Helen of witchcraft. I, in my wretched cowardice and deceit, did not speak the truth of what transpired between us, and thus, I became complicit in the false accusations and the wrongful execution of Mistress Helen and others accused of witchcraft.

"May God and the heavens bear witness to

my confession and my penitent soul.

"May God, those I have wronged, and the line that I bear forgive me for my silence in the face of evil."

As I finish my confession, I feel the weight of a hand upon mine. I hear the pressure of lips against my ear, sending a chill down my spine. Though I cannot hear the words, I know the voice of my ancestor. I close my eyes and see Elspet, walking through a field of heather. The cross that hangs from her necks is the same that rests on my collar bone. Her tartan skirts are hiked up as she marches toward a door surrounded by light. Behind her are my brother and grandmother.

My husband calls my name, and I open my eyes, knowing the news he carries. I know Grandmother has passed, but I also know she is not gone from me. She will visit, and I will not turn away the signs of her presence.

I have crossed the threshold of that door too, and I am no longer afraid. I know that Grandmother's prayers protect me, and I will protect my children, and the children who come after them, with my own prayers. I will pass down to them the wisdom of forgiveness, and the iron cross necklace.